Beauty became the enemy!

By

Mr. Umang Ohri

WP

WIZARD PUBLISHER

What's your story today ?

WIZARD PUBLISHER

www.wizardpublisher.com

ISBN: 978-81-949076-7-1
Hardcover: 299/-
Paperback: 199/-
Library of Distributor Number- **F2AB-HZA4**
First paperback edition: **February 2021**
Edited by **Editing Team Wizards**
Cover art by SJ
Layout by Ayaan Asif
Photograph by Team Wizards

Printed by **Wizard Publisher** in India
Wizard Publisher
B-109, R.G. City Centre, Jhandewalan, New Delhi- 110055

The story starts ~~from~~ in London [England]. When everybody was waiting for New year, 1969 had gone and 1970 was coming. There were ~~a~~ happiness and joy and– people were waiting for ~~12 o' clock~~noon. Everywhere there was a bustling of sound and Market were filled with crowd.

In Mean, While Lisa was waiting for his father. How much time ~~Dad takes~~does Dad take Already half an hour left? She was just grumbling Suddenly one hand put on her shoulder and she got screamed and move Back and said who is this? It's me your dad sorry I got late. She gasped oh, dad when your habit of frightening everybody will be going. Oh! Sorry My Sweet Daughter You know your stepmother If I ~~not took~~did not take a present for her she will get busted And I got late because of taking her present, and dad what you get for me? this is a surprise and I am not revealing this time and you will be waiting till 12.

OK, dad Let's go it is only half an hour left in 12. Ok, let's go.

"There in Lisa's house Melisa and her son waiting for him". He always got late but today he knows that there is ~~a~~ the last day of this year and tomorrow the beginning of New year and still he getting late Mom I think Dad is busy ~~in~~ shopping for Lisa You are ~~absolutely~~ right my son Your dad loves Lisa more than us. **"After all she is her first child."**

Hey, Melisa and Adam Oh! You come back I thought today you would not come and stay outside and celebrate the New year with your daughter only Oh! honey, again you start to see what I brought for you. A beautiful dress and for you my lovely son I bring a new brand watch Wow dad such a great watch Thanks a lot dad it's a wonderful gift for me and Lisa what's your dad bring for you? I think it's much better than my present Oh! Mom my present is not so good ~~from~~ as yours even he not takes any gift for me It's just for you and my little brother How sweet of you Lisa.

OK-OK everybody come together It's time.

"There is a ~~12 o' clock~~noon on watch and noises of the cracker gets started and firework brightens the sky Everywhere there was a sound of Happy New year Four of them were happy they wish to each other But who know~~'~~s what this year takes".

"In Early Morning Howard enter ~~into the~~ Lisa's room and summon her slowly." Lisa- Lisa Oh! Dad **'In grunt'** what happen it's 6 ~~o'~~ o'clock and today is a holiday Please let me sleep No Lisa wake up to see what I get for you, what s' Dad? Wow, such a fabulous dress you brought for me?

Lisa, you understand why I couldn't give this gift to you in front of your mother.

Because she shall start giving bullyrag And I don't like this so I concealed it and waiting for morning Thank you, dad You are great, Yes, my daughter I am ~~really~~ sorry I can't stop your mother to always humiliating you. My Hand gets bind because everything is in the hand of your mother This was my biggest mistake in my life that I gave everything to your stepmother.

Oh! Come on dad she is good but she is just grumpy and still, she is a ~~Well~~ Well-Wisher of us and I know she loves me but she doesn't want to express it. I hope you are right but yes today **"I came to know one thing that you are not only most beautiful from the outside but also from inside."**

Hey, Howard wakes up.

It's 9 ~~o'~~ o'clock. Ha-Ha Happy New Year My Sweet darling same to you Howard. I couldn't think that you brought such a beautiful dress for me Thanks a lot, but I think you don't trust me. No honey, I trust you but one thing comes up in my mind that you are not brought anything for Lisa- this thing not digest me Oh, come on You start doubting at me again, sweetheart you know that how much I love you, and today we are going outside for dinner only me and you.

So, in the evening I will come early and we shall go That's great honey I wear that dress which you gifted me on that dress how do I look like? Gorgeous.!

Come on I made ~~a~~ breakfast and today I make special for everybody Adam, Lisa, Howard come to the dining table the breakfast is almost getting cold. Yes, Mom, Adam come and sit here, where is your sister? I think she is sleeping Ah! She is so sleepy I already said that don't wake up late at night and Now we are waiting for a queen.

And what about your dad? An hour ago, had been calling him and still, he is not come "**She comes downstairs**" Hey Lisa I know you would be sad because your dad didn't take anything for you and I thought that you are not coming for breakfast. No mom you are wrong I am absolutely fine. That's good sit down and have ~~a~~ breakfast So, what's you make mom? A Cup Cake that ~~looking~~ looks delicious. **"I eat with relish"** Of course my dear eat as much as you want- after all this is the only thing which you get in this house properly.

What's going on between the mother and daughter Oh! nothing mom just shows ~~to~~ me her love that's great Lisa ~~After all~~, After all, she is your mother and she should get a chance to love you yes honey? Yes, you are right Howard! Adam why not you take more cupcakes? No Mom I don't want to eat more otherwise I get fatty.

Oh! My dear, what you eat just only 10 cup-cakes you should take more, No Mom it's sufficient for me Hey mom can I have one more? No, you already had eaten so much Lisa take it from me, no dad please you eat.

Oh! come on Lisa! Your mom doesn't make ~~a~~ special food every day

It's very funny.

OK Dad I am going Now But where? Just hang out with my friend's OK Bye- Bye My Dear take care. Mom I am done with my breakfast now I am going ~~for~~ to roam OK Adam Go and have fun Bye Mom, Bye Dad Your son doesn't have any work just roamed outside I don't know when he did study.

You always said bad about my son and what about your daughter she doesn't think about family She roamed here and there and go ~~for~~ to parties & she is not even thinking about her age. She is so beautiful anybody can easily attract ~~over~~ her and She doesn't have to care about it. And what type of friends she made? have you look that her friends ~~Is~~ Are look like ~~a~~ jail-break prisoners? first, you have to haul your ~~own~~ daughter then say anything about my son.

Oh! honey, you get anger I am just joking It's fine I stop my daughter but please don't do Quarrel See today is ~~a~~ the first day of New Year and I don't want to waste this day in fighting and ~~in~~ Obsolete word So fresh your mood and be ready I came at evening and then we go for dinner.

Come on Smile Melisa I say you again don't say anything about my son understand. OK - OK I promise lady ~~hitler~~ Hitler What? Nothing Bye Sweetheart sees you ~~at~~ in the evening.

"In coffee corner Lisa's friend Wanda and Jessica waiting for her." Today again she gets late Had you gave her time? Yes of course Wanda I told her that we meet her at ~~12 o' clock~~noon and see it's around 1 pm. I don't know when her habit of getting late is gone I think she gets somebody in her path and she goes for a date after all she is so pretty.

I think you are right Jessica **"does she lack ~~of~~ boys"?** ~~Everybody~~ Does everybody want to be-friend Hey girls what you are talking about?

Finally, you came. We thought that you would be going ~~for~~ on a date with somebody Oh! come on you ~~really~~ think that I like anybody it's impossible Ok we see about its Happy New Year Lisa, Same to you both.

Have you ordered anything? No just two coffees we were waiting for you. Ok come on I feel hungry Mom made a cup-cake but she didn't eat me too much So please order fast. Your mom still not like you? I don't know Wanda but I think she still jealous ~~with~~ of me. What the reason behind that I couldn't find out.

I can't say anything to her because of my dad She holds everything of my dad's property because of that she does whatever she wants Today if my mom is alive, she never let this happened. My dad did second marriage because he wanted that somebody takes care of me. But he didn't know that the outcome of second marriage will be this.

Oh! come on Lisa don't feel sad everything will be alright the time is not the same. Now forget about this look our pizza has come Let's take enjoy of pizza Yes.

Hey look over their Eddy and his friends come So what! everybody can come there is no restriction for anybody. I know Lisa you don't like him but you do not see he is so handsome and charming If you like him why not you propose to him, Wanda. Oh! come on Lisa everybody knows in the college that Eddy only likes you Whatever.

Hey Lisa what a co-incidence you are here Hey Eddy what's up I am fine and what about you Wanda & Jessica and you sweet girl I know that you remembering me and see I am here. Hey, girls Tom and Marcus both of you also here Yes Eddy wants to give us a party that's why after all he is wealthy.

Hey, Lisa you also here? Yes, hi boys Hey you don't say me Hi It's fine why not you say me Happy New Year Ya--Ya Happy New Year Eddy Aa Not like that why don't you like me every girl in the college loves me and you are the only one who doesn't love me. See what crunch I have? I have everything good personality, money, motor-bike all and still you not like me Eddy I know you have everything but one thing you don't have Sincerity, Politeness, Kindness & Respect.

I don't like that type of person who doesn't have this major quality You just use the girl and when you feel bore you just throw ~~then~~ them just like the **obsolete** thing I am sorry to say that but I don't like that type of people who just fulfill their sexual desire. Lisa! You come on the verge of my impatient just tell me who filled the bad **resentment** in your mind about me. Hey, Man calms down It's ok she doesn't know about your look Tom what she said to me? I said truth because I saw and everybody knows your truth so please You! Hey, stop Man.

Lisa come with me but Wanda Lisa please before the situation is going to be worse, we have to get out of here Ok take me with you otherwise I don't know what I do. Hey, calm down Man look everybody see us She made a joke in front of everybody they will ~~definitely~~ pay for this Nobody can refuse my offer or proposal What she thinks that she will go on like this by insulting me.

"She has proud on her beauty I will break that Proud & Dignity of her I vow to myself Until & Unless I put her down, I never sit comfortable Mark My Words."

I know you are Relentless & got Madcap when you get angry but please shun their word, she ~~doesn't~~ isn't capable of you why you wasting your time on that come on Man Appease yourself. If you are not my friend then I break your mouth, Marcus! I think Marcus right you don't need to burn your blood for that girl if you want to take ~~a~~ revenge ~~from~~ on that girl then you have to wait.

You are right Tom you are the only one who understands me & nobody else I also care for you Tom just only exasperate you It's not right that we do anything wrong with anybody. I think you should discuss it with her and solve your problem Oh! come on Man Eddy is not a child who just go and talk with her. You do not saw that she humiliated- and slandered him in front of the peoples and you said we don't do anything and put a hand on hand & sit.

But enough Marcus I don't want to listen to anything You just leave I don't want that guy who eats my things and Humming the other's name Ok fine I leave but remember you are not doing a great job, Eddy. You do not need to listen to him he is a coward and he always screams from everybody but you are Man and you never let anybody ~~to~~ get away with this Hmm.

"Tom~~m~~ succeeded in Trick & Deceive to Eddy. And he left the coffee shop what the outcome of this?"

On west minister bridge what you need to ~~fought~~ fight with Eddy you know that he is a bad guy and egoist person his father has a lot of money on which he roasting and bullying others Lisa you didn't do a great job. Oh! come on Wanda I am not afraid of this type of people I am strong besides you and Jessica with me. Yes, ~~definitely~~ we are s with you but you think what happens if he does something wrong with you or with your family.

His father has a big connection and He can do anything No-No I know his father you have ~~a~~ wrong thinking about him he is an innocent guy and ~~kindfulS~~ kindly He is ~~totally~~ different from his son; he is down to earth person and they achieved everything from his hard work. Eddy never understand because he never does any hard work But I came to know that Eddy's father prostitute somebody and trapped him in his house for a long time. Oh! come on Jessica you still believe ~~on~~ in ~~a~~ stupid news he always tries to defame the reputation of the wealthy and respected people.

And he even knows me personally and I know when I again telling about him, he ~~definitely~~ takes any action against him Don't faith so much ~~on~~ in anybody Lisa I ~~have~~ doubt that his father knows everything about his child.

But one thing comes up in my mind why you hate him so much? He loves you and he always ~~try~~ tries to make you happy then Why? You never tell us.

Come on Lisa we are your *friend* just share your past with us Ok-Ok I tell.

be*f*ore I met with both of you in college on the *f*irst day, I met with Eddy he ~~was~~ also took the admission ~~on~~ at the same time He was decent & nice and he also stared at me *f*or a long time. One day I went to him and asked his name? he said his name is Eddy and ~~you~~ I said My ~~Name~~ name is Lisa. We talked together and when we became a *f*riend, I thought he is loyal and he never does any wrong with me ~~like~~ as the other boys do~~es~~.

He ~~not loves~~does not love *f*rom the outside but *f*rom inside also and Not like the others who want to be a *f*riend *f*or just lying with me and he only loves my body and doesn't want to understand me *f*rom inside That's why I maintain the gap with the other But Eddy was not like the other He told me that without my permission he never touched me and misuse of me.

But one day there was a Christmas party in the college Everybody was thrilled and drank and Me and Eddy was also drinking so **much, Suddenly** I *f*elt discom*f*ort and I said Eddy I think I am not *f*ine are you okay Lisa I think you drink so much so we should go to the hostel room. No, I want to get back to my house No in this condition I can't take you to your house.

You stay ~~to~~ in my room today and tomorrow I drop you at your house I said no but he emphasis me so I agreed He took me into his room and I lie on his bed and he also sat down with me.

I woke up and asked what happened you don't want to sleep he said today is a spectacular moment of our life and we are wasting them in sleeping that's not fair what do you mean Eddy? Suddenly he grabbed my hand and said come on! Lisa today we made this moment memorable and he started kissing me. I tried to stop~~ped~~ him but he couldn't suddenly I thrived him and tried to get out ~~from~~ of his room but he holds and propelled me into his room.

Why you afraid Lisa there is nobody and today we make our relationship even stronger I said I am not ready but he ~~not listened~~ did not listen Look Eddy you drank so much and you promised me without my permission you never touched me oh! come on Lisa this is not a perfect relationship for me Just talk and talk Now I bored from this come here today we write a new story.

Eddy, I never thought you are like that No I have to go and I got up from ~~a~~ the floor and again open the gate but he caught my hair and I shouted in pain Aaaa.... And he threw me on his bed.

That moment was such a terrified and I started scaring and beg him please Eddy stay away from me but he didn't listen to me at all and he grabbed my hand and started again forcefully kissed me suddenly I saw a vitreous glass kept on a table. I took that glass and slammed it over his head and He fell ~~down~~ on ~~a~~ the floor and the blood came from his head and I open the locked and ran away. I came down-stairs and rushed to the hostel gate Watchmen asked what happened but I didn't answer him.

I came back to the college where the party still going on, I drank a glass of water and sat down Miss Venica saw me and came to me what happened Lisa you went to the hostel with Eddy why you came back? No mam everything is fine I am alright Are you sure? Yes, Miss ~~Venica~~ Venice. Ok, Lisa After that incident I never met him. He tried so many times but I never gave him a chance That's why I hated him so much "**Lisa started wept and both of them consoling her**" I never thought that he is just like that, he is a beast and evil.

I am sorry Lisa No we both are sorry to you we always thought that you were in your ~~own~~ ego but Now I came to know that why you always maintain the gap from the boys because we never knew that what type of bad resentment going on in their mind No Wanda & Jessica you are my best friends. Today by telling you all this thing My weight on my Heart gets lighten. One thing comes up in my mind Have you ever tell this thing to your father? Not at all, I know My father is my best friend but still I am always afraid that if I tell him about this what he will think about me and by mistake, if this thing gets to know by my step-mother She will not leave me anywhere.

Yes, I know but seriously I never knew that you had so strong & tuff otherwise if there any other girl instead of you she has broken. Yes, you are right Wanda I agree ~~from~~ with you Lisa you are great No-No I am not great I do what I think it's right. Hey had you ever did anything about this like told anybody or take any action against him? Yes, I always thought that I must let him ~~realised~~ realized his mistake but I can't reveal this otherwise it divulges in public, and because of fear of insult I had decided to talk to his father.

Personally, that's why I know him he was such a ~~kind~~ kind-hearted person when his son did with me then he scolded him in front of me and made me believed that he will never do again but this guy is just like a dog's tail never get straight. Ha – Ha if he doing it again then what you do? Then I am not holding me and hand over to the police after that whatever the outcome. Ok – Ok let get over this here see there is almost time and we should go to our house ok Lisa can we drop you No I am going by myself.

Are you sure? Yes. Ok, Wanda & Jessica have a good day bye Lisa tomorrow we meet. Hey mom I am back Hey little boy when did you ~~came~~come. Before 1 hour and you where were you roaming Huh just a coffee shop and you, I know you would hang out with your girlfriend. Oh! come on Lisa don't tease me you know there is no girlfriend You not make me fool younger brother I know everything her name is Christina Am I right Adam?

How do you know them you are keeping an eye on us? Hmm No but I have some detective everywhere who watch you all the time. Very funny look please don't tell anything about this especially to mom & dad because Christina is the daughter of Mom's friend and if she gets to know about this then she goes over there and talks about me & her future. You know the mom's habit! Christina is rich and mom loves the money more than us So that's why.

I know very well but in return, you have to do something What? You ~~organise~~ organize the party at home and invite everybody because you have ~~a~~ better taste and I want that everybody gets impressed.

Are you crazy party at home It's impossible if mom came to know that what will she does with us? You don't know oh! come on Adam mom not allow me but you can easily take ~~a~~ permission because she loves you and she never procrastinates your words.

So, I request or I even beg you - you can't do a little thing for your elder sister. But Lisa you don't understand the scenario If Mom & Dad come back so early and she seems your friends then she creates ~~a~~ big trouble and gets you out ~~from~~ of the house. I am not afraid ~~from~~ of mom you just take ~~a~~ permission and after that, I will handle this Ok fine Lisa Hey! Mom Honey where you have been all this day Nothing just here & there.

Have you not enjoyed or you didn't have enough money to spend if you want that I give you No Mom I am just asking one thing can you please allow me to do the party at home? What but why! I mean why you need to do the party at home? you know a lot of dirtiness spreading here & there and who clean the house? Had you remembered the last party one of your friend drunk so much and after that, he disgorges all the time and I cleaned that I knew mom but this will ~~be~~ not happen again I swear this is not your mind I think Lisa told you to ~~said~~ say me because his friend also present in the party.

Tell me the truth Lisa said you? No Mom do you ~~really~~ think that I obey Lisa's word Never I dislike her and their friends also and by calling his friend I ~~am~~ do not perish my party. I just do because today is a New Year and I show everybody how much wealthy we are and make my friends green with every.

And of course, this will also increase your reputation and when you sit around your friend, they just make a bridge of compliments Seriously mom! I speak the truth please Let me do the party Please- Please! Ok – ~~Ok~~ ok you can do the party but there is one condition After the party you have to clean the whole house and the most important thing that Lisa's friend shouldn't be ~~seem~~ seen ~~in~~ at your party is that clear.

Yes, mom but what about Lisa where she will be going? don't worry ~~about~~ that you need somebody to serve your friends Am I right? but

Lisa Is my sister and I can't let her do this. Listen, Adam! Lisa is your stepsister and she never loves you besides your father also doesn't loves us I put ~~a~~ control on your father and your sister otherwise they are throwing from his house.

So please don't be humble for your sister you just stay away from her Ok Mom Good Adam you go now I have to ready before your father come **'Adam enters into ~~the~~ Lisa's room'** what happen has she agreed to do the party at home? Yes, she agrees but she put some conditions that your friends don't allow in this party. Oh, don't worry about that I manage and thank you ~~my little brother~~, my little brother, you did a great job I just only did because you black-mail me besides I also want to do the party so that's why.

What you plan? we have to do a lot of preparation so; I go and buy something for the party and you decorate the whole house Fine Adam but what you said to mother? why you going outside when you already went. Don't worry I will think about it Before going I call Wanda; I give her great news Wanda picks up a call Hello Lisa Hey what's up! Have you done something? nothing you tell today there is a party in my house What! wow, that's great but your Step Mom allowed you? I remembered that she didn't delight~~ed~~ ~~of~~ in being her ~~in~~ at the party. Na she still not gives ~~a~~ permission then Lisa? My brother took.

Mom thinks that Adam does the party but this party is ours and you know Adam doesn't like the party so much but if your mom gets to know about- it? oh! come on Wanda you always get afraid you just call other friends and tell ~~be~~ me on time ok I have to do a lot of preparation so bye Wait -Wait! What the time i~~t~~s 7 pm. Ok.

Wanda call Jessica Hey Jessica what's up! Are you busy? No what happens everything is all right? yes of course I have to say that Lisa ~~organise~~ organizes the New year party at home. Wow, that really "**over the moon**" But her mother agreed ~~for~~ to this didn't she do any argument against the party? No, she didn't tell us about the party.

But then Wanda? her brother took the permission from her mother he said that he wants to do the party and her stepmother allowed him That's mean she disguisedly does the party and pretends ~~like~~ that her Brother's party's going on but ~~actually~~ that will be ~~the~~ Lisa's party.

Yes absolutely! Alright, I get~~s~~ ready for the party and I wear today a new dress which I brought yesterday. What you wear Wanda? please don't wear that usual cloth change your sort of mind. ~~Have~~ Has your mom or dad given~~n~~ you any new dress? No at all you know my Mom & Dad both of there are a miser and don't want to ~~spent~~ spend a single penny of money. And what's about your boyfriend Tom hadn't he gave you anything? he gave me an expensive watch I said him why you brought so much expensive watch for me? he said that you do not need to worry I got it ~~by~~ with my bestow money.

And I already spared a lot of money from my job but I said you not earned so much and what happened when your father gets to know about this? he just killed you He said you always get panic who said to my father? and I told my dad that doesn't interfere in my life So just relax! That's great he ~~really~~ loves you so much Wanda Yes. Ok, I cut the call Jessica you please inform everybody yes, I do Wanda.

Later ON. Hey honey I am back, where are you? hey dad what's up I am fine and what about you how was your day? Awesome dad. Had you enjoyed yourself with your friend? of course dad and you know today I ~~organise~~ organize the party at home. That's great but your Mom? I already agreed with her we told a lie that Adam doing the party but ~~actually~~ I does. Oh! She wouldn't know about this. Yes – Yes. May I bring a glass of water? of course, I am a little bit tired ok dad I get. Honey come on it's time yes -yes wait for a while I just get ready.

Sir have you inside may I come in? yes of course Hey Sam you here is there anything important? yes, there is one crucial paper you didn't sign~~ed~~ and you came earlier so I decided to visit ~~to~~ your house and get sign by you because tomorrow I have to submit this paper ~~in~~ to the bank.

That's fantastic you are my great employee you take everything seriously It's been no longer when you become a manager in our company! thank you ~~sir~~, sir, for your appreciation come on sit down Sam. Lisa, please bring two glasses of water? Sir, It~~'s look~~ looks like that you are waiting for somebody? Yes, ~~actually~~ me and my wife going for ~~a~~ dinner today and after that, we are also going ~~for~~ wandering.

Have you decided on any special place? yes, there is one famous restaurant his Name is **Chelsea Fun House** a three-floor restaurant. On the first floor, there is a bar where you get old drink & beer, and on the second floor, there is a dance floor where you dance with your couple and finally on the third floor there is a beautiful table which keeps vicinity of the pool.

And you can also take of enjoyment by seeing the wonderful scene of London You are right sir I also heard about it but I came to know that It's too expensive! I know but what is the benefit of earning so much when I did not take my family ~~on~~ to wonderful and stunning places. Hey, why not you take your girlfriend over there? she will ~~really~~ impress. I know Sir but I can't afford this besides she is fine and she never insists on me to take me ~~in~~to these expensive restaurants we are happy ~~in~~ with what I earn that's mean your partner ~~are~~ is ~~really~~ wise and loves you. Hello Mr. Sam Hey Lisa what's up? I am fine dad have ~~a~~ water thank you and you also have thanks. I also made a cup of coffee wait I bring for you No – No Lisa I don't have much time. I have to go and sir also getting late No I already made coffee and don't worry about My Mom she ~~is~~ does not come till 1 hour we have plenty of time but oh! come on Sam when my daughter insists you so much why not you have a coffee she makes a great coffee Ok fine sir.

'I bring a coffee' Sir if you don't mind can I say something? yes of course. Sir Lisa is so beautiful and so kind seriously if somebody gets that type of girl their life gets ~~totally~~ change. 'Here the coffee' Lisa Adam call you to go into the room and see what he needs? ok bye, Mr. Sam enjoy your coffee yes sure Lisa. What happens? wait I come. ~~Actually,~~ ~~y~~You are right Sam but I always afraid for her but why sir?

she is so courageous and strong from the inside and you should proud of that type of girl you have. Your all things are right but you have to think from father's side my daughter is so beautiful and ~~innocence~~ innocent anybody can take a benefit of her and you know the today's environment you don't know what the second person holds inside and her mother put a big responsibility on me. And when she had ~~took~~ taken her last breath I remembered she grabbed my hand and said please take care of my daughter she is different from others I am sorry that I am not with you and what the vowed we took at the time of marriage you have to keep further. And she closed her eyes~~-~~ and ~~on~~ at that time everything got finished after that I wouldn't take care of Lisa properly sometimes I forgot to take back from school, washed their clothes~~-~~, helped ~~in~~ with their homework and not even fed a good food because I too busy in my work and it's very difficult for me to manage~~d~~ both the house & job so I had decided to do marriage again.

And I met with Melisa! she was new in our office her Mom & dad were against and she was also in a living relationship but she was not happy with that so we became a friend and when this friendship became a relationship we didn't know and you married with her exactly Sam.

I thought that my decision takes a lot of joyness in my Lisa's life but ~~what~~ I know that this decision just only filled grief & sorrow she never takes care of my daughter always scolding her and I couldn't ~~did~~ do anything because my hand got bind ~~because~~. After all, her father is a lawyer and he threatens me that if I leave her daughter he put a liar case on me and put me into ~~the~~ jail, and ceased my all property. That's why I couldn't say anything and let it happened everything I always hoped things will ~~be~~ get better but it's going to be ~~more~~ worse and for changing the environment ~~on~~ in my house I also started pretending ~~like~~ that I ~~not loved~~ did not love my daughter and I love only her but she never hates me.

Even a lot of things happened with her but still, she loves both of us I always said you ran away from this house and never look back. I secretly meet you but she always says that don't worry one day everything will be alright and step-mom also will get change. So, you see my daughter went through ~~from~~ a lot of things but she never lost hope Sometimes I think about what she made of? and then I get the answer that she is going over her mother.

She had also that type of attitude ~~what~~ that Lisa ~~have~~ has she also never lose hope even in our bad circumstances she always courage me to pathos ~~me~~ and said everything will be alright.

"Don't weep!" Mr. Howard, it's such a wonderful story and I feel lucky that I am the one who listens to this Please sir don't get your mood off I pray to god that whatever the stumbles & ups & down come in Lisa's life ~~she~~ gets more happiness comparatively to them. She never cried but I know I always see whenever I enter ~~into~~ her room ~~in~~ at midnight she always cried on the bed and I didn't even wipe out her tears. What type of dad I am? and I feel ashamed ~~on~~ of ~~me~~myself. No sir doesn't blame yourself this wasn't your fault you just changed ~~the~~ Lisa and your life but what we can do with luck it's all that fault.

You just did what you think it's better Now sir please don't cry wipe out your tear see it almost time Mam can come anytime and if she sees you like this- then she starts asking the question now I think you know much better than me. Ha-Ha-Ha. Please sir sign this paper can you please give me a pen? Ok Where I sign it here at the bottom Sir Ok Sir, I leave now wait Sam have you complete that report you know I have to show him tomorrow. No, I don't get time but I start at night and it ~~have~~ has been completing since morning Make sure you complete it If this successful then we get a big surprise

Yes, sir why not have a nice day. Hey! Honey how long you stay in the room we already getting late. Why ~~you shouted~~did you shout Howard? I am coming I had been waiting for you ~~since~~ for 1-hour Melisa so what Howard? Have you don't see that I get a ready look how's my dress sweetheart? It wonderful, stunning I don't have a word for this. And How am I look like in this dress? baby, you look sweet in all dress when you wear even an ordinary dress that's become ~~a~~ special. Oh! ~~really~~ thanks a lot, Howard Ok fine Melisa let's go we are late Lisa Adam come both of you Yes dad? please take care of the house May-be we come ~~on~~ in Morning so that's means the whole night we are outside of course! honey but what about the house I can't leave the house on both of him especially Lisa.

Oh! Don't worry mom I take care of myself and Adam- ya – ya I see Lisa and Adam you remembered what I said in the afternoon If any trash looking in my house you have to be ~~clean~~ clear that yes Mom I knew and I also keep- an eye on Lisa she can't call anybody you please to go with dad and have ~~fun~~ fun, Ok Honey! Let's go Bye. Bye, dad takes care of both of you.

That's great Mom & Dad gone now we do a party but Lisa we don't decorate house till and in less minute how we can do that? oh don't worry I already prepared everything I went to the market and buy all the snacks; juices dad already knows about my party. What you told dad? of course Adam what you think about how I get arrange of ~~this~~ these things Dad secretly put some money in my pocket and this was dad's plan to took mom wandering the whole night so that we enjoy without any worry. I never think dad would do this so what you think about dad Adam? Come on! Adam, we don't have much time they will arrive ~~in~~ at any time and we make all arrangements here Let's do it.

Put the light over there Hey Lisa. 'Wanda & Jessica come' I feel so glad to see you we came so early because we thought that you need some help that's great "the more hand we have the quicker the work will be". Put a table over there Wanda all the juices keep on the table and Jessica please pull the sofa over there & Adam have you hanging all the lights of course and what about you? You just ordering us and not doing any work oh! hello, I manage everything here. I think you shall be a manager thanks for your compliment Jessica Hey look Lisa the guest starting arriving I go up and get ready will you please both of you entertain our friend?

Yes, Lisa you just go and get ready what you wear today? this is a surprise Jessica but come on I want to know oh! come on Jessica why you resolute you just ask like a stubborn guy. Wait when she comes down, we all can see Ok fine Wanda Hey Wanda & Jessica How are you? Hey, Helen what's up it been a long time we do not saw you.

~~Actually,~~ I wasn't here Then where you were Helen? I was going outside ~~the~~ London Wow that's fantastic but where? Mauritius you know my boyfriend, he is wealthy and he always took me here and there. He spends a lot of money ~~at~~ on me, see a diamond ring he gifted me ~~at~~ last night It's looks so expensive Wanda How much it is? it too expensive ~~in~~ which you can buy a wardrobe of dress "There is a need of asking Jessica." I attended big parties where a lot of rich people come to This party is cheap for me But I love Lisa and I couldn't break her heart that's why I came here Ok you enjoy Helen. Have a drink? of course, where's the drink? keep over there. ok, I take it. She is always show off that's why I don't like her. Hey Wanda have you call Marcus & Tom also?

Yes, after all, he is also our friends and you don't forget that tom is my boyfriend and how I enjoy without him. But it's not our party It's Lisa's party don't you think Lisa feel bad when she came to know that we called Marcus & Tom here. She doesn't like this after all he is the friend of Eddy Oh! come on Jessica we can't judge all ~~on the basis of~~based on one person and I believe ~~on~~ in Tom he never like eddy he is ~~innocence~~ innocent and he always stays with me and never thinks about any girl other than me.

And as far as Lisa's concern don't worry, I make her understand and I know she understands us Ok Wanda as your wish! Here ~~the~~ Adam's friends also? of course Jessica this party is for both of them. Christina Hi. Hey, Adam what's up! I am fine and what about you? I am good So, you finally ~~organise~~ organize the party Adam ya but there is one secret behind this? What I held this party for you baby. Seriously you ~~not said~~did not say liar Not at all this party is just for you Thank you so much ~~Adam~~, Adam, That's my pleasure but I want to ask one thing that these all are your friends? I have never seen it before.

No this is My sister's friends. Oh, ~~actually~~ my sister insisted on me so much and you know me that I am ~~kind~~ kind-hearted so I couldn't say no but I told her that your friends did not interfere in my enjoyment. Your sister obeys you I mean she is elder than you but still, it's fine Ok you enjoy the party Christina look there is a lot of drinks over there come on ~~have~~ having one with me. **'Everybody is in fun'** Hey Wanda

Tom I knew you come here of course sweetheart I have to ~~here~~ hear after all you called me. Hey, Wanda Hey Marcus How are you I am fine and how are you Great as usual Lisa ~~organise~~ organize the great party Ya~~—~~- Ya where she is? she is in the room to get ready Ok Tom where you have been all this week? I called you So many times. What I said to you ~~actually~~ I stuck in work you know my dad without putting me in any trouble they don't get the peace I am ~~really~~ sorry but how much time she had to ~~went~~ go into the room? May be Jessica half an hour I think she should come when everybody- everybody asks about her.

But Marcus Hey looks Lisa come down. Hoooo....... ~~Wow~~ Wow-what a beautiful dress she wears! ~~Absolutely~~ Man! Wow, she looks like an angel in this blue dress She sparkling the light everywhere. That's why she is the most beautiful girl what you think Marcus? I ~~really~~ don't have a word for her. Tom, Can you please stop **praising** her? Oh, Wanda why you get jealous you are my great love always but I can't hinder myself to praise her. And even Nobody here who does not think about her Wow Lisa you look so pretty in this dress Thanks Jessica No she is right you are looking **Ravishing, appealing**. Thank you, Tom, but I wouldn't be called you. I called Lisa! you are nice looking thank you so much Wanda if you call him ~~than~~ then ok. Hey Marcus you look Handsome thanks for your compliment and what I said for you-you are looking heavenly.

Oh, thank you a lot Marcus. This is a nice compliment Why don't you have some snacks & drink Yes sure Hey Lisa Helen you are looking fabulous Lisa Thanks You are also not looking less Helen. Oh, come on I can't compare myself ~~from~~ to you No it's ~~nothing~~ anything Helen ~~by the way~~, by the way, Lisa who gave you this vibrant dress? ~~actually~~ This dress is given by my father. Wow, your father's choice ~~are~~ is ~~really~~ fantastic but one thing whatever the dress you wear you always looking nice. Have you taken anything? of course Lisa.

Hello Ms. Beautiful Ho – Ho look who is here Mr. Ben Don't call me Mr. just call me Ben oh – oh why I do not call you Mr. you become a big guy and you never meet me. Have you taken any news of me in all these weeks? By the way where you have in all these weeks? ~~Actually,~~ Lisa you know I am a scientist I have to go for research and I was busy ~~in~~ with ~~an~~ important research that's why. What was that research just tell me ~~actually~~ it's secret & confidential that's why I can't disclose but I will tell you It's my promise Ok As your wish whenever you want to tell.

So How did you know about my party? ~~actually~~ Jessica called me Had your call start reached? Whenever I called you- You had been engaged all the time So, I leave to call you. ~~Actually,~~ Lisa my phone had been working for two days and coincidently Jessica's call come and she told me about your party so I think it's ~~a~~ the right time to ~~apologise~~ apologize for my mistake so I come here and you can see I stand in front of you.

Lisa, I am ~~really~~ sorry it's ok Ben you were busy ~~in~~ with your work and it's more important than me But I feel good that you are here so tell me where you were Roaming? First of all, I went to Korea ~~than~~ than Japan, and last New Zealand. Wow, you wandered the whole world! I also want to roam the world and want to explore new things After my studies I also ~~took~~ took that job in which I have to roam~~ing~~ in different countries.

Why are you waiting for a job? when I true your dream You roam with me also Lisa Seriously Ben! Of course, I ~~really~~ want you to come with me and I ~~really~~ feel happy but don't you have any trouble because of my presence or you distract. No Lisa No you are my inspiration whenever I felt desperate, I starting thinking about you Your beautiful face comes up in my mind Whenever I get angry, your gorgeous smile appeases me from inside and whenever I feel sad your jokes just put a smile on my face.

So How could you said that your presence put ~~a~~ trouble Oh! I never thought that you felt like that about me Ben yes Lisa! ~~actually,~~ I don't know it's ~~a~~ the right time but I ~~really~~ love you. What! Hmm I mean just give me a time it ~~really~~ shocking for me No Lisa you don't put ~~a~~ stress on yourself You take ~~a~~ time even I also have taken a long time to say you this. So, I think it's a good time to propose to you Hey Lisa why you sit down like this Hm nothing can you please bring me a glass of water? Yes sure. Take "she gulpy drink". I need some time Ben right now I am not in the condition to give you an answer for this It's fine Lisa I told you I will wait to Excuse me I have an important call.

Hey, Lisa what happens to why you do not enjoy your ~~own~~ party? ~~actually~~ Wanda & Jessica Ben propose to me What! Seriously I mean when did he do that? a few minutes before.

So, you don't like her but Jessica I feel Nervous I mean after this incident My mind not let me get into the other stuff, and another thing that I don't know much about Ben. But he was your school friend Lisa yes Wanda but we not met properly with each other even in ~~the~~ school also and suddenly he came and proposed that ~~really~~ strange. And might be I not loved him the way I loved Eddy Oh! Lisa, you still think about Eddy forget him just like he is a bad dream, and think about your future Ben is a good guy and everybody is not the same just give him a chance to ~~proof~~ prove himself and if he passes then you go ahead with your relationship otherwise you stop yourself. It's not a big deal look Lisa till when you stop yourself to make a relationship? someday you have to need somebody and ~~on~~ at that time your partner will support you so calm down and think about it.

I think you are right how long I stop myself to love somebody or being a partner of somebody Thank you so much ~~Wanda,~~ , Wanda, you open my eyes No problem anytime now forgets everything and let's enjoy hey Lisa have you arrange any music? of course Lamp. I play ~~a~~ the piano How? but do you know how to play the piano yes, I already took some classes. ? Hey Lisa ~~if you don't mind,~~ , if you don't mind, can I play first Yes, Tom why not go-ahead Tom – Tom It's really fun when Tom plays the piano ~~of course,~~ , of course, Wanda had you know about Tom's this skill. No, I see the first time.

Oh! It's not strange that tom didn't tell you about this No I don't think so. Okay. Okay, Tom bro Now see here the book of music and I hope I do not forget this it has been a long time ~~to~~ since doing the practice ~~of~~ piano. Let see ting tong ~~ting tong~~..............

Hey, tom do you ~~really~~ know how to play this? yes, my Sweetheart just waits again Ting Tong....Ting...Tong.

He plays strumming ho---ow Is there anybody who play the piano properly? of course! Lisa here Heyyy.... Your sister knows How to play the piano yes, she plays well. Lisa -Lisa... everybody cheers you Lisa go and play piano ok Jessica.

'She goes near to piano' will you please yes sure Lisa I am sorry I don't know how it is happening it's ok Tom "**sometimes our ~~own~~ smartness not work".** You are right thanks for your suggestion, Lisa.

Hmm sorry baby I couldn't play that piano don't talk to me tom you just cut my nose and I don't want to create any stuff so please keep quiet

"Lisa started playing a beautiful melody music and everybody falls ~~down~~ in his ~~own~~ thought and lost in his ~~own~~ imagination".

'In restaurant' Honey you arrange a beautiful table I ~~really~~ like this Yes; sweetheart this is just for you Melisa you know since you came into my life ~~My life~~ get ~~totally~~ changed.

Really! of course, sweetheart lot of happiness comes ~~by~~ from your feet and you maintained my house very well I don't know what happen ~~with~~ to me If I ~~not m~~did not meet with you. Thanks, Howard, for your compliments I never know that you ~~really~~ think about me like that This restaurant is too expensive to have you ~~really~~ afford this? Yes, I am working on one project if it gets successful ~~than~~ then I got the promotion.

~~Really t~~That great! So, Melisa what you want to take? I think we should start with wine and some fried fish. Ok, waiter yes sir! What did I get for you? Please bring one red wine and fried fish.

Ok just wait for a while Howard can I ask one thing? Here ~~sir~~, sir, your fried fish, and red wine thank a lot **'enjoy sir'** Hey Melisa take your glass and come on cheers 'Gulp- Gulp!' Hmm, Its taste is sour. Yes, Melisa, this wine is pure and tastes this fried fish it's ~~really~~ delicious Howard, I don't know is the right time or not? But I have to talk. Yes, what do you want to say, Melisa? ~~Actually, y~~Do you know that Lisa's age is being married now Why not we look any boy for her? She is beautiful and young and it's our responsibility to get her to marry as soon as possible.

I always afraid ~~for~~ of her the way she acts I don't think that anybody likes her and I want that she married in a big house her husband is wealthy and always keeps her happy.

What do you say? You are right Melisa but don't you think we do fast, do we? She has the right to take our own decision we can't force her to do what we want whenever she wants to marry, she can and look that what's the age of her it's not enough to marry. Yes, you are the only well-wisher of her and I am nothing No Melisa I am not saying that you are not her well-wisher but we can't take this big decision without her consent. Oh, come on Howard you are always favo~~u~~ritism of her. Lisa is this! Lisa is that! I also think about her that's why I said that I am her mom and I always have concern for her.

I know but don't do any argument with me I already make up my mind and I know that Lisa will never refuse me. Ok, fine Melisa we talk later on Can we continue for which we are here? Yes sure.

'~~In~~ In-**home everybody enjoys and time is almost 1, o clock**.' Lisa, I think we should go wait for Wanda & Jessica why are you going so earlier? no Lisa look at the time and you know my mom & dad start questioning if I have gone late. Thanks for a great party goodnight Lisa goodnight Wanda and you Jessica what's your reason may be you are escaping from helping me in cleaning my house. No Lisa ~~actually~~ Wanda told me to drop me My house come in across the path of her house so that's why but we had planned to do the party till morning but what can I do now ok goodnight to both of you.

'Everybody slowly-slowly left the party.' I think ~~my~~ only a few friends are left but it seems that they have also started going but look at ~~the~~ Adam's friends they don't even bother about the time it's almost 3 am.

Adam- Adam! What happens Lisa? ~~you dru~~did you drink Adam? who allowed you to did this leave this Lisa what do you want to say? have you watch your time why not you saying your friends to leave? How rude you are Lisa your friend is gone doesn't mean that my friend also goes and besides I took the permission of this party, not you. Had you remembered Adam what the mom said to you before she came all house should be cleaned.

Oh come on Lisa when you grow up and why you obey our mom? she doesn't even love you and always said wrong about you- ~~always~~, conspiring you behind your back and you know what mom said to me that she plans for your marriage so that half of the property which is the name of you directly get to the name of mom.

What! Hey Adam come here ya I am coming to Lisa I have to go wait – wait for Adam what did you ~~said~~say? Whatever you told me are they right? Mom ~~really~~ plan for my marriage but how can she do this to me? I never teased her she did a lot with me but I never said any word to her and endured everything She can't ~~take decision of~~decide my life like this.

Whenever she will come back, I talk to her Hey Lisa what happen to you looking depressed? no Ben nothing just tells me Lisa have you troubled because of my words? No Ben you just leave me right now but Lisa please Ben I don't want to talk please leave me. **"She goes upstairs and gets into the room and closing the door".**

Hey Ben what happens everything is alright why Lisa ~~gone~~ went upstairs and close the door like this? I don't know Rik I think her health was not good might be she worked so hard that's why it's happened. And what about your proposal she accepted it or not.

No, she didn't answer yet Don't worry Ben Lisa is a good girl and how you proposed to her everybody got shocked just give her ~~a~~ more time I think you are right Rik but maybe she hide something but ben it can be positive also. Maybe she made a plan~~ned~~ to give you a surprised the way you gave to her Yes you are right. **"After all the fruit of patience is always ~~be~~ sweeter".**

Ha-Ha-Ha let's go Ben it's almost morning ok.

"Lisa look at the mirror" I never did bad with anybody but why is the god doing with me always? When I starting loving ben then this would ~~be~~ have happened but I not let this happen with me anymore I fight for my rights She always acts like a dictatorship in this house.

She thinks that she rules over every life but enough is enough Ok Lisa calm down and sleep tomorrow it's a big day for you Mom if you were with me this time you never let this happened with me, I ~~really~~ missed you. Dad always takes care of me but I always felt lacked ~~of~~ you and he always said I am very strong and have ~~a~~ great endurance and all the qualities you had it is all in me but I think I only have 1 percent of this. But When the big challenge comes in my life now, I get afraid to face it.

So how can I be strong but still I will be plucking up and talk to her somehow and I know that she listens to me after all she loves me may-be. Ok fine I wipe out my fear and get to bed I hope tomorrow~~'s~~ morning any miracle waits for me Ok good night Lisa.

In early morning Melisa where's the key here in my purse take Hmm **'the door open'** home sweet home. Look Howard how is the house everywhere trash and see the floor is colo~~u~~red with soup and what is this? beer can! was there any drinking going on? And my walls who dirt him. ~~Whole~~ The whole house is going to be a mess I told Adam strictly before I came everything must be clean but they didn't listen to me but My son is not like that I am sure Lisa would be responsible for this.

But Melisa you said No to Lisa for the party so how could she do this? Howard just keep ~~quite~~ quiet you don't know your daughter she is clever and she can do anything after all whom she belongs to. Enough Melisa you said what you want to say I have been listening to you longer and you just blame Lisa a~~n~~ beside you also say wrong to her mother don't forget to whom you said wrong they ~~was~~ were my first wife without any evidence or asking how can you prejudice anything. Don't you need to ask ~~from~~ Adam before you say anything You ~~gave permission to~~permitted Adam right~~.~~ ? Yes -yes, I am bad, you and your daughter never did anything whatever does it's me and son and don't shout at me alright don't forget that everything is in my hand and if I tell to my father what he does with you.

You can't imagine so please mind your tongue, Mr. Howard Ho! Honey, you get angry I just said why you burn your blood just wait for a while when Lisa and Adam wake up I ~~myself~~ asked him alright you just calm down Ok honey and if you take ~~a~~ favo~~u~~r of Lisa then seriously you ~~really~~ suffer that's my threatening to you.

'The Alarm Bells' Lisa open her eyes what's the time oh no it is 8 am I am going to late for college today.

But wait let us check everything is ~~a~~right in the house or not She open the door and see the whole house was a dirty lot of beer cans kept on the table and pieces of food were spreading everywhere and the whole house ~~is look~~looks like a garbage house if mom looks this scenario she bust like a volcano I go rapidly and wake up Adam. **'Lisa enter into his room'** Adam wake up man look you supposed to clean the house Let me sleep don't disturb me oh! Come on smart boy what can I do. **"She takes a glass of water and flashes over their Mouth"** what – what happen Lisa are you stupid what are you doing? I didn't have any choice you won't ~~woke~~ wake up so what a big deal in this Adam had you forgot what did you promise to mom? Look outside the whole house is dirty and you have to clean it. You are lucky that mom and dad do not arrive otherwise nobody knows what happens **"Lisa and Adam came out from**

the room" see oh! ~~My~~ The god I forget about this Lisa what I do now? Don't worry Adam if we do fast, we can clean the house before the mom & dad arrive come on first of all you take all the cans from the table and I broom here ok but where I keep these cans? I give you polythene wait Adam.

"Lisa goes into the kitchen and suddenly Melisa and Howard come down-stairs" what's going on over here? oh! Trying to rally up their mistakes Mom when did you ~~came~~ come back? 1 hour before my son and where is the planner oh!

What am I asking? she is sleeping right now and why not she slept she did the party the whole night as I see Adam here the polythene.

"She shocks" Mom & Dad you so what you expect who should here? Hmm, nothing Mom. What is this Lisa were you doing the party? No Dad when Mom said No to me How can I do the party? Wait for Howard I have to talk to her so Lisa you just act like that you always obey me but now the truth comes today you were just pretending. ~~You~~ Do you never respect your family have you ever feel what suffer at your family when we see these things? But mom shut up Adam I am not talking to you. You just keep ~~quite~~ quiet I come to you later on but this time Lisa answer me this party ~~were~~ was planned by you? Right, Mom hmm tell me yes great! How dare you ~~to~~ do this when I told you strictly that you ~~not did~~did not do any party at home you still **"Melisa slap on her face".**

What are you doing Melisa why you slap her? Oh, stop it Howard I did this earlier but I ignored her all things because of that their wings come out and she ~~fly~~ flies ~~on~~ into the sky. If I put her rein on her before then today, we not see ~~this~~ these things, you liar

Enough Mom Enough I endure a lot but now this time enough You **"She again ~~try~~ tries to slap her but Lisa grabs her hand and puts down"** Mom don't do this again otherwise I forget that you are my father's second wife.

What did you said Howard you see How's your daughter talk to me? Lisa No dad today I have to speak please don't come between us. So, mom now come to the point you said that you always think about me and if you put a reined on me then this day not came So, tell me what I did a wrong everybody has a right to do whatever and live the way they want and **"What you gave me always abuse and Humiliate".**

You never like me from the beginning and you never love me like the mom does I always thought that you never let me feeling short of my mother but I was wrong you always let me felt that I am your step daughter. Have you ever cared about me? Dad didn't have ~~a~~ time even he couldn't take care of me because of work pressure but you always busy ~~in~~ grooming yourself. When dad outside for a few days you didn't ~~gave~~ give me ~~a~~ proper food just gave me ~~a~~ stale food and even I had to wash~~ed~~ school cloth myself.

Whenever I went to school, I didn't take ~~a~~ lunch with me because you just busy with your friends and I spent the whole day with starve stomach and always let me to did the household work like washing dishes cleaning the house, etc.

You always brought a new thing for Adam but never for me I remembered my 12th birthday when you gave me an old and ventilated frock.

You always scolded me and expressing that Adam you and dad ~~is~~ are your only family and I am just an outsider. **"The tears come from Howard's eyes and Lisa speak in tear"** I am sorry but **"You just misused and prostituted of me"** And I also came to know that you are planning of my marriage but remember one thing I marry with a guy who loves me truly and I am not let you ~~to~~ take this important decision of my life.

'Lisa went into her room and slammed the door' Melisa Shockley sit down and start thinking about her How did she say to me like this? She filled with anger and grumbled. Mom are you okay No Adam don't go near her but why dad I said please just leave her alone you go and ready for your school ok dad. **"Adam and Howard left the** ~~drawing~~ drawing-**room and Melisa just sat like a statue".**

How could she do that? Nobody can talk to me like that where she got this much ~~of~~ courage, I have been always bent her in front of me Whatever I said to her she did and I never let her speak in front of me ever. But today her voice came out and its look like that **"She was not another else were".** I afraid that today she raised her voice and tomorrow what happens if she would be starting claim on Howard's property No – No Melisa I have to do something Lisa you not did a great job now I show you **"Who am I in real and I ruin your life no matter what".**

I will pretend that I am your well-wisher but in reality, I shall be the one who Dilapidates and Deteriorate your life

"Remember your beauty shall become your ~~own~~ **enemy this is my curse to you".**

'Lisa come out from the Room' where are you going and why you hang a bag with you? Dad, I am going to college and in this bag, I have clothes But Lisa are you leave this house? No after college I shall be going to stay at Jessica's house for few days. But this is strange you never went to stayed anybody's house and today you are? Dad, why are you worry I am just going to fresh my mood But Lisa wait for Howard if she wants to go then why you stop her? Melisa you know Lisa never stays far away from us and you know in today's environment everybody keeps an eye on a beautiful thing and try to misuse ~~of~~ him.

Oh! Come me on Howard you are very possessive ~~for~~ of her She is wise and she knows the difference between right and wrong Lisa I am ~~really~~ sorry for whatever I said to you earlier and whatever I have been doing with you. I knew you were innocent and want a love of mother despite ~~of~~ that I only just teased you Lisa I never saw ~~a~~ love inside you for me and you always obeyed me and tried to ~~made~~ make me happy but I was blind, I never tried to become a good mom for you And **"I have been just becoming a villain in your life".**

Your blames are ~~absolutely~~ right so I decided to give ~~me~~ myself a punishment today and for this, I just leave this house What! Melisa, what are you doing are you out of your mind? No Howard **"As much I**

criminal of Lisa I have yours also". Howard, I just took a benefit of your goodness even Lisa's also I am not capable for you That's why I make my mind and this should be happening with a bad woman like me **"Melisa cries crocodile's tear"** Lisa and Howard please forgive me for my wrong thing and rude behavio~~u~~r.

"Howard shock and think, ~~are~~ is she really change or she is just playing a trick with us let see" I am going now goodbye Lisa; goodbye Howard please take care of my son. **"Melisa walk to the door suddenly the voice come behind her back"** stop mom you don't need to go anywhere we both of us need your dad not to live without you and even Adam & I also. This house only runs because of you **"I forgive you"** Oh, thanks' sweetheart **"Melisa hugs Lisa"** I know you are a ~~kind~~ kind-hearted girl and have a great heart like your mother and You truly forgive your stepmother Huh? Yes.

Again, thank you so much ~~my princess~~, my princess, Now you have to go you are already too late for college and after that, you stay with Jessica as m~~uch day~~any days you want Ok Mom thanks! Bye, dad bye Mom.

I shall meet you after a few days **'Lisa left the house and Melisa sit ~~on~~ at the table and have ~~a~~ tea'** Wow Melisa you just win my heart today

Seriously Howard? Yes, my darling I can't imagine that you changed so quickly.

I don't understand how can it happen~~s~~? Do you have any doubt ~~in~~ about this Howard? No – Not at all But I was thinking **"How this much ~~of~~ love for Lisa come inside you"** You still not believed? No Melisa but I never saw you ~~to~~ love her. Oh! Howard, you still doubting ~~at~~ me Now my heart has been changing I ~~really~~ felt bad that it was I who did all these things. I always hurt her but she never said a single word to me Now when she revealed her sorrow then I ~~realised~~ realized everybody ~~have~~ has feelings and I never understand her properly. So, I try to recover everything **"That's ~~really~~ wonderful thought Melisa"** I hope this will be forever Of course, Howard Look what's the time go and get ready otherwise you are late for your office.

Oh my gosh! You are right honey today it's my important meeting maybe after this I get a promotion and become ~~a~~ the general manager of the company Oh! Wow, that's ~~a~~ great news Howard yes! You just pray for me ~~of course~~, of course, Howard, and after that, I ~~organise~~ organize a great party. Ok – Ok Now I go and get ready.

"In college" Hey Lisa what's up Hi Eva. How are you fine and you great So How was your holiday I listened that you held a party yesterday? Yes, but why you not came? I invited everybody. I am sorry but I went somewhere with my parents and you know my Mom ~~she~~ wanted me to with her on the first day so that's why Oh! It's fine hey have you did the project which ~~were~~ was given by Ms. Martin? Oh! I forgot that Now again you standing outside the class Lisa.

Have you done it? Of course, you know me I always completed my work and you know this project carries a grade also Hmm Eva.

Ok ~~Lisa,~~ Lisa, I have to go I see you in class Fine Now what can I do? she yelling at me if I do not show my project to her I had been not submitting any project to her and I remembered that she gave me a last chance and I lost him also. Hey, what happen Lisa do you have any trouble? yes, Wanda ~~actually~~ have you know about the project which ~~were~~ was given by Ms. Martin. Yes – Yes but I didn't do that project Even you also not did that but why ~~actually~~ I had been busy with my boyfriend ~~in~~ for the whole week and yesterday you held the party and I spent the whole night over there so I didn't ~~got~~ get time.

That's great if I get more people like you then Mrs. Martin can't do anything and in helpless she has to give us more time to complete the project but it's not possible to ask each and everybody separately.

Relax Wanda we have two and another is Jessica I know she wouldn't do the project and I believe that even the whole class ~~not did~~did not do it because almost everybody was in my house last night and besides who does the project in today's times.

Let's go the class ~~is almost start~~almost starts Hey Wanda, Lisa where were you both I had been waiting for Nothing Jessica we were just discussing ~~on~~ something Ok – Ok sit down to see I hold a seat for both of you. Thanks, Jessica you are great Hey look Eddy enter into the class so what! No Lisa looks something strange always three of them enter into the class Eddy, Marcus, Tom but today Marcus is not with him. Maybe he is going too late and come after sometimes But Wanda Hey sweetheart oh! Tom How are you handsome I am good and what about you and Hi Jessica oh! Look who is here the most gorgeous girl Lisa. Hi, Tom Hi Lisa How are you I am fine It seems that you are still angry ~~from~~ with me No Tom everything is fine and why I will angry ~~from~~ with you.

You do not do anything with me and besides if you want then you can't because you are not alone anymore Wanda is also with you now You are

~~absolutely~~ right Lisa that's why I like you so much Your great words always inspire me Thank you for your compliment, Tom.

"The time is 10 and Ms. Martin enters into the class". Hello ~~everybody~~, everybody, I hope you enjoyed your weekend and the first day of New year So, can anybody tell me what you did yesterday? ~~Actually~~ Ms. Martin Lisa ~~organised~~ organized the party at home and we all ~~were~~ went over there. Wow, that's wonderful Lisa forgot about the project but never forget about the party.

"Everybody laughs" Mr. Eddy what about you? you might be also ~~went~~ going to her party ~~after all~~, after all, she is your best friend Huh No Ms. Martin, she has not called me and I was busy yesterday with my dad. That's strange your best friend ~~organise~~ organize something and you did not go strange anyway! so everybody I hope you did the project along with the enjoyment.

"Lisa thinks" great Now Ms. Martin asks to stand up whosoever not do the project and the whole class is going to be stand up So~~;~~ before I say something stands up whosoever not do the project.

"Lisa, Wanda, and Jessica stood up but the whole class doesn't". Wow, what's a coincidence three of them but again Lisa **'Lisa think'** what is this why the whole class don't stand I thought most of them not did the project and the bad thing is even Eddy and Tom did the project. You three of them come out Wanda and Jessica can I ask both of you why you ~~not did~~did not do the project? Mam keeps quiet Lisa you don't say any word we talk in front of the ~~principle~~ principal enough is enough now.

Wanda & Jessica still gave me two ~~—~~ -three but you never submitted anything Always gave me stupid excuses but now I don't listen to anything you just keep your mouth shut and come with me I ask ~~to~~ both of you later on.

"Lisa and Ms. Martin going to the principal room". Wanda I afraid Ms. Martin was looking so angry Now what happens ~~with~~ to Lisa?

Calm down Jessica I listened that the new principal is good I hope so. But will be everything alright with Lisa? God, please help her.

Ms. Martin enters into the ~~principle's~~ principal's room" may I come in Mr. Casper of course Mam So why you here like this and who is this girl with you? Mr. Casper her Name is Lisa wow she is so nice and pretty I have been never seeing her in this college? ~~Actually,~~ Mr. Casper, she has been studying ~~from~~ for 2 years and this is ~~a~~ the Last year of her. Oh! So, what happen Ms. Martin? Mr. Casper, she didn't give~~n~~ me any of the projects from the beginning to the last year I told her so many times that you lost your mark but she does not listen to me. I had been giving the project to the whole class ~~before~~ for 1 week and said that submit me after your weekend and new year holiday and I strictly told her that if you do not submit me this project then I do not tolerate you anymore.

But again, she does the same thing I don't understand why the children do not take their future seriously So many times I told her that please think about ~~your~~ her future but this relentless girl never took my word seriously. Mr. Casper, I recommended you please take ~~a~~ strict action against her I think you should suspend her but mam please don't do this please give me one last chance I will complete my all project please Mam, please.

No not at all Lisa **"Now the water goes up the head".** Calm down Ms. Martin just calm down otherwise your BP gets high Look at her she is ~~innocence~~ innocent and, ~~in~~ at this age, they didn't know in which thing they have ~~a~~ goodness. But Mr. Casper it's ok you just go I talk alone to her and I make you believe that she will not be doing this again alright as you feel right Mr. Casper.

"Ms. Martin left the room and only Lisa and Casper were in the room" Lisa sit down here ok sir Look why you do this when your teacher told you this project ~~are~~ is crucial then why?

"Lisa looked hesitated" don't be hesitate Lisa just talk to me friendly Sir if I ~~be~~ am honest then I feel bored in doing this thing~~s~~ Afterall who do the project and my hand gets tired by writing such a lengthy project, I ~~really~~ don't like this seriously Hmm I think you are right Lisa but this won't be good in further.

Look this is the question of your career and I don't want that the sweet girl like you lose her career but whatever you did you should get ~~punishment~~ punished for this. Sir, I am ~~really~~ sorry I promise I never do this again but this time please forgive me **"Suddenly Casper grab her hand and indulgently put another hand on her back"** I can do anything for you Lisa.

"The way he touched her and sta~~r~~ring at her Lisa felt discomfort" What do you mean sir? Lisa when I saw you, I was just lost I never saw such a beautiful girl like you in my life. Yours one glimpse make my mind mad

"He squeezed her back and said," Lisa I make an offer **"If you spent one night with me"** I promise I will save you and I promote you without any giving exam and I change your whole life which you can't imagine **"What! She shouts and stand up furiously".** Are you out of the mind what you just said to me? look at your age I am your daughter's age and you talk to me like this shame on you.

I go now **"She just opens the door and he grabbed her hand again"** please Lisa! She leaves her hand and slaps on his face Now you got my answer Casper **"She opens the door and gone away". "Lisa wept and ran on the floor"** Hey Jessica look who is running? its Lisa! But what happened to her? I don't know Wanda let us see Lisa – Lisa wait what happen why are you crying**? "Lisa embrace Wanda" Hey – Hey come on just tell me to calm down.**

"Lisa speak in grief" The principal did a wrong with me What but How? He touched me wrongly and he said that if I stayed one night with him then he promoted me and forgive my all mistakes.

"Jessica in anger" that's the fragile guy I thought that he was a nice guy but **"He turns out to be in a sheep's skin"** yes you are right Jessica seriously how can he do that he just prostituted her. Lisa you don't worry we go to the police station and complaint against him No Wanda

I can't but why Lisa? You know Wanda he is a principal of the college and here its personality is a good and kind person and nobody can believe because I don't have any proof against him and besides if I did the complaint then it will be coming in the news and because of that there would be a lot of insult of my father But we can't sit quietly like this because of little bit insult you will leave like this Lisa? But Wanda! no Lisa Wanda is right **"It is not fair".**

Don't worry if we can't go to the police station then we go to the authority of this college My father has a great acquaintance in the authority I talk to my father regarding this You surely get the justice we shall rusticate that principal.

Jessica, I don't know how I do thank you to you Oh, come on!

Lisa, we are ~~a~~ best friends and don't forget that earlier you also helped me when I was in need and now when you are in trouble then how can I leave you like this ~~of course~~, of course, Lisa we both of us with you Thanks a lot to both of you. So today you will stay with me we are doing a lot of enjoyment Yes Jessica! **"Lisa looked upset"** come on! Fresh your mood I know it's not easy but if you lose yourself like this then how will you fight? Hmm, Jessica. Ok – Ok I know one place where we fresh our mood I listened that their food is amazing and a little bit cheaper also Are you saying true Wanda? If you do not believe Jessica then come with me Shall we go Lisa? Yes, ok let's go.

"In the office, the **meeting had been going on** ~~from~~ for **2 hour**s**"** so finally we came ~~on~~ to the conclusion that if we built a dam here then it's very easy and convenient for the people and the company gets more profit because of that our shares ~~is~~ are going high **"everybody claps great Mr. Howard"** well done Howard I knew that you are my best employee. Thank you so much ~~Mr. Anderson~~, Mr. Anderson, I feel glad that you like my work Why not you gave a great presentation Howard I ~~really~~ trust ~~on~~ you Thanks sir Ok everybody the meeting is over let's start work on this project and I feel pleased to inform you that your new General Manager of this company is Mr. Howard **'Whole cabin is echoes of with clapping'.**

Wow! That ~~really~~ wonderful I thankful to you sir I won't speak I can't able to express my feeling No Howard you ~~really~~ deserve this after all this is the result of your efforts and hard work And I also made you an in charge of this project ~~also~~ Double happiness oh god! How I handle this?

Relax Howard and ~~in~~ at the inauguration of the new manager I ~~organise~~ organize the party tomorrow and I invite you all to Come with your family yes sir sure So, everybody gets to work and Mr. Howard comes to ~~my~~ the cabin I gave you a few pending works which were left by old General Manager.

"After half an hour Howard enters into the cabin" May I come in Mr. Anderson?

Yes – Yes, I was waiting for you? Have you got the file yes Sir Hmm! What happens sir you are looking upset? nothing Howard. You can tell us ~~sir~~, sir, if you want after all we all are family You are right Howard you are the only one to whom I can share anything. ~~Actually,~~ I am ~~worry~~ sorry for my son he doesn't have a focus in their life I always told her that after me you are the M.D of this company but he never listened to me and said that I am not interested in handling the business & all. He just Wanders like a vagabond No stability, no consistency Even he is not good ~~in~~ at studies at all I got admission him ~~in~~ to the top of the ~~university~~ University of London but still, he remained unworthy.

As far as I knew you said that your child was an all-rounder and good ~~in~~ at ~~the~~ studying Yes, you are right Howard but it had been an old talk when her mother ~~leaved~~ left her that things put a bad effect on his mind and he always felt alone I never gave a time but fulfill all their demand and never let her sad You are right sir every parent got sad for their children even I also included in this.

I always thought about my daughter your story is the same as mine but the twist is that **"your son's mother, leave your house and My daughter's mother leave this world". "Howard eyes filled with tears but he wipes out"** you are ~~absolutely~~ right Howard but Now you can see what his age? I think I should do this? But what do you want **"Howard asked in surprised"** Marriage what! I mean really but your son agrees ~~for~~ to this? I know he will not agree but if I get a girl who is sincere, dedicated, and beautiful then he will ~~be definitely~~ agree. By the way, why you got surprised ~~actually~~ Mr. Anderson I am also looking for a boy for my girl her age is now 25 and I think the sooner she gets married the better is.

She is smart, sincere, relevant from inside and besides she is the most beautiful in whole London **"Mr. Anderson quiet for 1 minute and said"** Howard why not I should get my son married to your daughter?

What I mean Ho! Howard, I need a girl who change my son's life and the qualities which I looking already inside your daughter it will be so good that ~~me~~ I and you become a family not only in a company but in real also.

Yes, sir, you are right so say Howard are you agree? Hmm, can I talk to my wife before I take any decision? Of course, you don't need to worry you can ask your daughter also ~~after all~~, after all, it is crucial for her and she has to spent her whole life with my son. so, talk ~~in~~ at your home and tell me your final decision at tomorrow's party.

"Howard came out from the cabin and thinks" what did Mr. Anderson said that's right as far as I know his son, he is arrogant and egoist he can't keep my daughter happy. But I can't break the heart of Mr. Anderson after all he is my boss, he never treated me as an employee always treated as his ~~own~~ brother I am trap in ~~a~~ great confusion **"Howard gasped"** I talk to Melisa regarding this she is change now and maybe she gives me a good suggestion.

'On pizza corner' that's was ~~really~~ nice yes Wanda yes you are right and did you like It Lisa yes ~~of course~~, of course, it~~'s really freshen~~ freshens my mood I feel glad that I make you happy Lisa thanks a lot to both of you seriously you are my great friends Hmm.

Look who is coming in the car he is? Ben Hey Lisa, you are here actually I went to your college but I came to know that you were not in the college so I started searching for you and see you find here but why were you searching for me? ~~Actually,~~ Lisa I want to talk to you so can you please come with me if you don't mind Hmm No Lisa you go Me and Wanda get back ~~by~~ my ~~own~~ self.

Are you sure yes Lisa you don't need to worry you just go Ok Wanda and Lisa I am waiting for you ~~in~~ at my house and will you be getting back before the dinner? I shall be on time Jessica Ok bye both of you. **"Lisa sits in the car and goes away and Wanda & Jessica also go back to her house".**

So, ben what you want to talk about and where you take me? ~~Actually,~~ Lisa, I can't speak in front of your friends that's why I took you like this ok fine but what you want to say? Lisa had you remembered that what I said to you ~~in~~ at the party? That I like~~s~~ you and I want to ~~spent~~ spend my life with you but ~~on~~ at that time you were not in that condition to give my answer and it's obvious because everything has happened so suddenly now I think you can able to give me an answer so Lisa do you love me? ~~Actually, b~~Ben in all these days lot of things occurred even my stepmom's plan for my marriage because of this I wouldn't think about your proposal.

What! Your mom plan for marriage but from whom? I don't know ben but I strictly said that I will marry ~~with~~ that guy whom I like not to your choice of guy Ok so you don't like me, Lisa? No, I am not saying that but I need a little more time if you don't mind ok great ~~actually~~ I ~~organise~~ organize a dinner party in a famous restaurant tomorrow so you come ~~at~~ for dinner and then you tell me your final decision I think its sufficient time for you because I shall be~~en~~ waiting for your answer from a long time and now I can't wait so much so, please. Of course, ben I tell you tomorrow I hope your answer ~~are~~ is yes and I text the address of my hotel where I stay Ok ben So, can I drop you at Jessica's house yes Ben ok Lisa **"In evening ben drop Lisa at Jessica's house"** ok Lisa goodbye and please think about us.

Of course, ben you are a nice guy and whosoever live with you never get sad but it's the question of my life and for me, it's a big decision I hope you understand Yes Lisa I always see you happy and whatever the decision of yours that's agreeable for me So, goodnight Lisa Goodnight ben.

'Lisa enters ~~into the~~ **Jessica's house and everybody sat** ~~on~~ at **the dining table and waiting for her'** Hey! Hello everybody oh! Lisa, I felt ~~worry~~ worried about you I thought that you were stuck in some kind of problem no Jessica you forgot that I was with ben and he was picked in front of you Oh!

Sorry, I ~~really~~ forgot about this so **"where is your story going"**?

Ha – Ha – Ha. Nothing Jessica! Hey, Jessica let her get in did you take everything over there? OH! Yes dad, come in Lisa we were waiting for you? Hello, uncle hello Mrs. Pot wait I go and take a portion of food for all of you. Ok, Mom Jessica why not you sit no I go and help mom you just sit and relax **"Jessica goes into the kitchen"** so Lisa how are you I am fine uncle what about you. Great!

So, what's going on everybody alright in your house your Mom, ~~dad~~ Dad, and your brother yes, they all are absolutely fine That's good ~~actually~~ I want to say that Jessica told me the incident occurred with you and I talk to you regarding this. I felt really bad when I listened to this, I immediately took an act on and I suspended that principal from the college and even took ~~a~~ legal action against him but you have to go to the police station for some information yes of course uncle I don't know how I thank ~~to~~ you. No ~~Lisa,~~ Lisa, you are just like my Jessica and besides, if this ~~is~~ has happened with my ~~own~~ daughter then I also did the same.

But uncle you do a lot for me nobody does this for anybody Thanks a lot you are such a great guy No. no nothing but Lisa whenever you need anything you ~~are~~ feel free to ask me.

Yes, uncle sure **'The dinner is coming'** great keep it on the table ok dad **'Jessica sit at the chair'** today mom made a special dinner come on! Lisa ~~have~~ has it of course you also take Jessica so dad had you told Lisa about the action taken by you? Yes, we were talking ~~on~~ about this before you came great, I hope you feel better now Lisa yes Jessica thank ~~to~~ you.

You did a lot for me no Lisa doesn't ~~said~~ say me thanks ~~after all~~, after all, we are best friends and I am available anytime Ok – Ok everybody please eat ~~the~~ dinner they are getting cold. Ok, dad.

'In Lisa's house' hey honey I am back, where are you? I am in the kitchen Howard Please bring a glass of water for me **'Howard sit ~~at~~ on the sofa'** Take the water thanks sweetheart So, Howard how was your day? yaa - awesome and there is good news I became a general manager of a company. Wow, congratulation honey I pray to god today that you get a promotion and see you got it now the celebration must yes of course Melisa. Wait I bring a bottle of champagne now today we celebrate with this **"Melisa gone to the kitchen and brought champagne" "the sound of pop up"** so honey it's the name of your new post cheers **'Both of them drink the glass and sat at the sofa'** today is a big day for both of us we have been waiting a long time for this.

Yes, you are right Melisa Hmm But what happens Howard you look upset you are not happy? ~~Actually,~~ I want to discuss something what Howard? You know Mr. Anderson who is the owner of our company yes ~~of course~~, of course, Howard you told me but what happens? Hmm actually Melisa ~~he~~ was disturbed ~~for~~ by their son's marriage and I also said that we were also looking for a boy for our daughter. Then Howard? so he said that he wants my daughter ~~gets~~ to get married to his son what! **'Melisa shock'** Are you serious yes of course Melisa Wow that's ~~really~~ great! My daughter will be going ~~in~~ to a big house today god gives me ~~a~~ double happiness.

I was stumbling here and there finding a good relationship for her and see the proposal himself come by walk I know I would never get a good relationship like this. So, Howard when we talk to Mr. Anderson? He

~~organises~~ organizes the party tomorrow so we will talk over there because he said to me that I gave my final answer to him ~~in~~ at the party. It's ~~a~~ big news Howard so why not you call Lisa and say to come ~~in~~ to the party tomorrow? But Melisa but what Howard? you don't think we do just hurry I know his son he is not good at all even he not respect anybody besides their father also and ~~in spite of~~despite that how can I say yes to Mr. Anderson for this marriage and we not even asked Lisa about this before answered anything.

We should ask first **'Melisa got irritated and shouted Howard!'** what happen, Melisa? **'Melisa quickly change her expression'** I mean Howard you just think where we get this type of good relationship and after marriage everybody gets change and our daughter has so many skills by this, she can make good anybody. And don't forget Mr. Anderson also lives in that house if something gets wrong then they can handle it and he never let her sad.

But Melisa you don't understand Lisa has to spend her whole life with his son and Mr. Anderson not live all the time with him And I came to know that **"He did wrong with one girl in the hostel".** But because of the power and money of Mr. Anderson he ~~not ca~~did not come in the news

He does not stick on one girl then how can I say yes and **"Perish whole life of my daughter"** *just for* a small designation. **"This thing is not more important than my daughter's life" "Melisa starts thinking this stupid guy ruin everything because of his foolishness and after her marriage the money and prosperity we get all going into drain No – No I have to do something".**

Oh! Howard, please sit here look I know you worried even I also but try to think Mr. Anderson is a big and wealthy guy in the whole London and he also kind-hearted person and might be because of small age somebody gets instigate his son that's why he went on a wrong path. But think about it if ~~a~~ the right person comes into his life and telling him what is right and what is wrong then he gets ~~totally~~ change and I am sure Lisa is the one.

Who put his son on ~~a~~ the right path and fill good resentment inside him She has power to victory on anything and I know My girl **"she is born to rule"** And everybody will bend in front of her and I know **"she goes in that house for ruling not for serving: mark my word".**

You are right Melisa but oh come on! Sweetheart you think so much tell me his son come ~~in~~to the party tomorrow Yes, Melisa ok you meet his son and if you think anything wrong ~~about~~ with him then you say no to Mr. Anderson. But I must say that we don't get this chance again Ok Melisa you say then I met his son but if I get any wrong then I won't late to say No fine Howard now you go and fresh then we do dinner.

'In Jessica's house, both are in a room' hey Lisa did you like dinner? Of course, Jessica but why are you asking this?

~~Actually, m~~My mom ~~not mad~~did not make a delicious dinner at all and Me and my dad always turn the nose up when she put ~~a~~ dinner in front of us that's why. No seriously Jessica she made ~~a~~ good food today I think Lisa it happens luck by chance "**both of them laughs**" Ok – Ok Lisa but where Ben took you? ~~Actually,~~ Jessica, I told you that ~~ben~~ Ben proposed to me at the party yes Lisa then? He came there for my answer we were not going anywhere just wandering then Lisa what did you said him I know – I know you say yes to her am I right? **"Jessica ~~leapt~~ leaped on a bed"** No – No Jessica ~~actually~~ I got hesitated and in hesitation, I couldn't ~~said~~ say yes to her What! Lisa are you stupid how can a girl like you afraid ~~in~~ of saying something?

Lisa, you are lucky that you get ben he is a nice guy and I saw that how much he cares about you when that incident happened with you then I told ben about this and you know what he does? He went to the college and grab his collar and smash a fist on his face.

Wow! I never thought that he could do this Jessica yes Lisa even I also Jessica you are ~~absolutely~~ right I shouldn't do late he invites me for dinner and over there I will say yes to him that's my girl Lisa. hey, look your phone ringing Lisa whose call is this? It's my dad

Hello dad how are you I am fine my heart you tell me great Sorry I disturb you Lisa No – No dad you can call me anytime but why do you call me at late night everything is alright? No everything is alright Lisa I just remembered you that's why I call you. Ok, dad what's about mom and Adam both of them are good?

Yes, they both are fine Lisa I want to talk ~~on~~ about something I know it's not ~~a~~ the right time but it's ~~really~~ crucial for you that's why Yes, dad but what do you want to say you tell elucidate. ~~Actually,~~ Lisa, there is a marriage proposal come for you what! I mean from where dad? Lisa this proposal is given by Mr. Anderson who is the boss of my company. He wants your hand for his son Mr. Anderson! Lisa, what happens do you know them? Hmm no dad Lisa I understand that It's so ~~hurry~~ hurried but I said to your mom that whatever the outcome comes the final decision is yours. He gives me one day time and he invites us ~~in~~ to the party which is tomorrow so Lisa do you come to the party? **"Lisa gets shocked and confused"** dad ~~actually~~ I never tell you but this is the right time to say you I like one guy. What! Who is this guy? Dad, he is Ben He was my school's friend but you never tell me before Lisa? Dad, even I came to know this time that he likes me and ~~I~~ me also.

If you like him then definitely, he is different from others and ~~really~~ a nice guy **'In your happiness my happiness is Lisa'** So, do you not come to the party? No dad he calls me for dinner tomorrow so I will go over there. Ok ~~Lisa,~~ Lisa, I got my answer and I am happy you choose your partner to own yourself so, enjoy and I want to meet him before you take any decision further Of course, dad for me your decision will be final that's my good girl ok my little princess good night, good night dad.

What happens to Lisa what was he saying? Nothing Jessica, you tell me to come on **'Jessica insist'** actually he was saying that there is a marriage proposal came for me and this proposal is given by Mr. Anderson. What! But Lisa you know Mr. Anderson his son was who did a wrong with you why not you told him. I can't Jessica I came to know that he is my father's boss and if I telling the truth then it creates a lot of Ruckus and what impacts come on his relation we can't imagine. Hmm, you are right but Lisa you can't conceal this truth longer yes but I will reveal at on right time Jessica but this time no Ok Lisa whatever you think ~~it~~'s good but I want to say one thing **that "Don't do late that one day it's too late"** yes Jessica thanks for your suggestion now I feel sleepy let's sleep because we have to wake up early tomorrow.

'Howard lie on a bed and Melisa enter into the room' Howard have you talk to Lisa regarding the party tomorrow? Hmm yes, Melisa ok what she said? She will not come to the party but why Howard? Have you not told her about her proposal yes Melisa I told her but she likes somebody else and she has a date with that guy tomorrow. What! But who is this guy? Howard and she never told me about this guy His name ~~are~~ is Ben and Melisa do you know he was her school's friend But Howard you know the today's boy "**where waives girl see no avail**". Oh, come on!

Melisa ben is a good guy and besides Lisa likes him and if she like him then definitely, he is something else.

Howard are you out of mind without knowing him how can you believe him so much ~~on~~ in that guy and Lisa is a child she doesn't understand the world but you have seen the whole world but still, you do this I can't believe this. Melisa why you get so ~~exciting~~ excited to do her marriage with his son when I told you about him listen carefully, I do what is good for Lisa and I not let any sorrow and pain come to her life and where's my daughter happiness my happiness is over there So I ~~take~~ make my decision I will say no to Mr. Anderson for this proposal.

'Melisa start thinking' everything will be perishing now I thought I get lots of prosperity, hono~~u~~r, and money but because of this foolish guy and her daughter everything is a slip from my hand there is no way now Melisa why you wake up No – No Howard I just sleep now.

In the morning Lisa wake up Lisa please let me sleep Jessica oh come on! Girl ~~it~~'s 10 am and you said that you woke up early in the morning but you do not wake up now look I get a tea also. **'Lisa wake up'** thanks for the tea Jessica its ok Lisa so today what you dress up? I have been not deciding yet But I get something for you wait **'Jessica open the wardrobe and get a beautiful strip dress'.** Here Lisa this is what I got for you wow such a fabulous dress Jessica but when did you get this? ~~Actually, t~~This is your birthday~~'s~~ present but I forget to give you I remembered last night about this so I take it out. But seriously this is ~~really~~ amazing you solve my problem today I wear this Thank you so much ~~Lisa~~, Lisa, you look stunning in this dress and why not today is an important day of your life and hey have you get the message ~~by~~ from ben? No Jessica ben not message anything tills but he sends me anytime.

'suddenly the phone ring' hey look Lisa something comes in your phone **'Lisa checks the phone'** look Jessica there is a message.

Let us see who send this? its ben **'Hey Lisa how are you I hope today I get my answer and it~~s~~ will be favo~~u~~r of me but Lisa I want to say one thing that whatever the answer of yours but I always love you no matter what I stay in great Britisher hotel and my room no. is 127'.** Lisa, what happens what is it? It's ~~the~~ ben's message ~~Jessica~~, Jessica, wow what he wrote in the message? He gave me ~~an~~ the address of the hotel Great Lisa when shall you go? I will be going at 5 pm because I think I take a present for him what do you think Jessica? I think it's a good idea Lisa he feels good when he sees the present and he will come to know your answer. I don't think he is so smart Jessica **'both of them laugh'** Jessica Lisa come to the dining table the breakfast is ready Mom hailing us come on Lisa we go for breakfast then we talk further about its ok let's go, Jessica.

'~~In~~ In office' so Howard how do you feel to become a general manager of this company? I mean sorry sir can I say, you Howard? **'Howard laughs and gently slaps on his shoulder'** oh! Bryan again you joking you know you are my best friend and whatever the post I am I always be your friend. Had you remembered Howard we both started working in this company together and see it has been 25 years and we are still here.

Yes, you are right Bryan how can I forget that the first day when I started my work here everything looked so strange on that time nobody talked to me properly but then you met me and after that, we face all the challenges together.

Yes – Yes Howard but one thing you agree that you were always better than me look you become a general manager and I am still a manager of this company I put my all effort gave my all-time but what I get just a small post. No – No Bryan you think the wrong buddy I get this post by luck I know you did more hard work than me and you brought this company ~~at~~ to the top and without you, I couldn't do anything and even I didn't believe that I became a G.M.

So please Bryan don't let this thing come up in your mind Howard you are right but I ~~really~~ feel disappointed all the time I just thought that one day I shall achieve everything in my life and when the time came all the things go far away from me. **'Howard ~~try~~ tries to console him'** No Bryan you are great and I know one day you go at the top Hmm Howard I hope you are right Howard sir Mr. Anderson call you in the office, ok you go and say I just come ok sir. Ok ~~Bryan~~, Bryan, I talk to you ~~later on~~, later on, I have to go I think~~s~~ Mr. Anderson needs something ok Howard we will talk at lunch.

'Bryan has gone and Howard goes to ~~the~~ Mr. Anderson's office' Sir may I come yes Howard come to Sir do you need something? No – No Howard you just sit **'Howard sat down at the chair'.**

Howard, did you remembered what I talked to you about yesterday about marriage? Yes, Mr. Anderson of course but you said that I give my answer ~~in~~ at the party Oh! I am sorry Howard I just forgot about this I hope your answer will be positive. So, Howard your family come to the party, right? Yes, sir but my daughter not come but why Howard she is most important, and without her how can we talk and go further. ~~Actually~~ Mr. Anderson **'Howard thinks'** this is not the right time to tell I tell him in the evening– ~~Sir~~, Sir, she is not feeling well but she gave her answer to me and I will reveal in the party in front of your family Ok – Ok Howard never mind we can meet her later on also.

Yes, sir any other thing you want no Howard just give me that file so I have to sign It's kept so long Ok.

'In Jessica's house it's around 4 pm and Lisa gets ready' how much time you stay in the bathroom Lisa it's half an hour you have been over there just wait a little while, Jessica. **'After 5 minutes Lisa came out from the bathroom'** wow Lisa you look stunning in this purple strip dress Thanks Jessica for your compliment No – No seriously today ben gets to fall ~~down~~ over you when he sees you. **'Lisa laugh'** what a joke!

So, have you decided what you buy for him? No Jessica you suggest I think you should buy a shirt for him.

Hmm no Jessica I think he has already had lots And besides who remembered the shirt may-be after some_time he not used it or he forgets about that hmm you are right Lisa now you tell what you want to give **"anything which is remembered always stay in front and never forgotten".** I think you should give him a watch it's always rememberable, stay in front and never ~~forgotten~~ forget I think it's a good idea Jessica seriously you have a sharp mind So, I decide I buy a watch that's good Lisa.

Ok – Ok Lisa you just go and wear a dress it is almost 2 ~~o'~~ o'clock and you have to buy the watch also Yes; you are right Jessica I just go ***'After 15 minutes Lisa came out ~~from~~ of the bathroom'*** wow! You are looking gorgeous you look like eight wonders. Thanks, Jessica I never thought that I will look so much ~~beautiful~~ beautiful in this dress No – No Lisa you are wrong I told you ben ~~definitely~~ fall down today Hey Jessica, Lisa! Wanda great to see you thanks Jessica wow Lisa you look fantastic in this dress. Thanks, Wanda so anything special why you wear this dress? ~~actually~~ Wanda Lisa goes for a date what! But with whom Jessica? It is Ben Hmm Lisa you didn't tell me about this.

~~Actually~~ Wanda this would ~~be~~ have happened so rapidly even I didn't ~~knew~~ know about it Whatever but I ~~really~~ feel glad that- today- you ~~are~~ finally come into a relationship and the good thing is that he is your old friend Yes Wanda you are right I never thought that My school's friend becomes my partner.

Hmm Lisa look at the time you must leave now otherwise you will be late ok I met with both of you later on and Jessica thanks for your service oh! Come on Lisa but wait you will not stay with me at night may-be! Jessica, you are stupid when she goes for a date then you ~~really~~ think she come at night both of him spent the whole night together Yes, Wanda sorry! Ok, I go bye both of you bye Lisa take care and enjoy your date.

'In Mr. Anderson's Mansion Eddy shouted' where's the park it been a long time to ~~told~~ tell him to ~~brought~~ bring a glass of wine for me and he still not come sorry sir I got late actually the stock had finished and I went to the market to buy them.

'He pushed him and he fell ~~down~~ on the ground' Make sure that you don't do this mistake again now leave **'Mr. Anderson enters into the Mansion'** what happened what kind of noise is this? Dad why you keep these lazy servants? He doesn't even know that what kept in the house or what-not? You just filled their stomach nothing else.

What happened eddy just tell me? ~~actually~~ I told park to bring a glass of wine for me and it's been ~~a~~ two hours to said him and when I asked him then he said that the stock finished.

So eddy what's a big deal in this not all the time the thing is available but dad relax eddy why your anger so much? just sit with ~~me~~ my look I can do anything for your happiness my son and put anything on your knees but dad you couldn't do anything about that girl. Oh, come on! Stupid boy you still burn in the Vengeance I told you when the right time comes you do whatever you want no dad it's easy for you to say but not for me you never care of me you just speak.

Eddy – Eddy you are my life and you don't know when somebody doing wrong with my life **"what I do with him"** just wait and watch **"one day you get a chance and nobody can stop you mark my word"**. Whatever dad! Ok, eddy listen today I ~~organise~~ organize the party and there is good news I fixed your marriage what! But dad with whose and whom you asked to did this? come on! Eddy, I am your dad and I don't want anybody's permission to do anything and besides, she is a nice girl and the good thing is that she is the daughter of my employee and you know very well it's Howard what! Mr. Howard, he has a daughter! But he never tells us even I didn't know my son look I find him very difficultly so I insist you to please come to the party and met with him Is she also coming ~~in~~ to the party? No Eddy but I told Howard to give his answer ~~in~~ at the party.

No Dad I shall not come ~~in~~ to the party and I am not interested in this marriage and look at my status I marry with your employee's daughter what's the status of that employee in front of me I am the son of a wealthy person and he is just a Hackneyed guy But son try to penetrate enough dad I don't want to listen to anything my decision is final.

Eddy ~~gone~~ went out ~~from~~ of the house what a stubborn child he is ***'Mr. Anderson thinking'*** what I do know he refused the proposal and he will never accept at any cost but I can't say this to Howard otherwise what reputation of me in front of him? He doesn't give his answer yet if he says yes then I make him agreed So stop thinking and let's look after the preparation where's he going on.

"At 4 ~~o'~~ o'clock Lisa came out ~~from~~ of the shop" finally I get a watch it's too difficult to ~~chosen~~ choose the best watch but now everything is ok so where I get the taxi its 4 ~~o'~~ o'clock but he gave me a time at 6:30 so what if I arrive earlier so I give him a surprise and the expression come on their face will be awesome.

'Lisa call the taxi and by thinking this thing she sits into the taxi'

'Here eddy met with tom' Hey eddy what up! Bro fine ***'Eddy was looking upset'*** What happen you are looking sorrow is there any trouble? Nothing tom nobody cares me, nobody thinks about me No eddy I always with you in any situation why you think like that? I know tom but what I said about my ~~own~~ father he decided my marriage without asking me what! But ~~how~~ now it's possible eddy I thought you said that your father never took any decision without you.

Yes, you are right tom but I don't know what happened to him he just got mad, and why not! All the empire is in their hand no Eddy you are wrong your Dad loves you might be he would do it after some thinking but what! Tom, it's not important more than from my life I strictly said him that I will not do the marriage.

Eddy just calm down you do whatever you think it's right just given him a time maybe he shall ~~realise~~ realize his mistake and he leaves that decision I hope you are right Tom otherwise he shall Repentance on his decision.

'Lisa reached to the Hotel and came out ~~from~~ of the taxi'. Finally, my searching is over I get that person who loves me from inside not only from outside he not like my body he like me. ***'Lisa enter ~~into~~ the Hotel and gone to the reception'*** Hello mam welcome to Great Britisher Hotel how may I assist you?

~~Actually,~~ I have ~~a~~ dinner today and I have to go to Room No. 127 its book on the name of Ben.

Let me check mam yes there is a person name Ben booked this room so mam can you please tell me where this room? Yes, mam you just take the lift and go to the 5^{Th} floor and when you will reach the room is on the right side. ***'Lisa enter into the Lift and reached to the 5th floor'*** where's the room no. 127? Huh! here but the room was open he did not know anywhere? But how it is possible I wasn't informed him and nobody can say to him.

It's ok let enter ~~into~~ the room ***'Lisa enter and started calling the name'*** Ben- Ben ***'Suddenly some voices came from another room'*** What type of voices is this let us check ***'Lisa went over there and see that one person sits beside ~~the~~ Ben" "She just started calling him suddenly that person speak'*** you make her foolish well after all she trapped into your web.

Of course, Shane I never know that she would be so stupid She thought that I loves her and I will never touch her without her permission what ~~a~~ rubbish! But ben why you did this drama I don't understand? ~~actually~~ Shane Lisa is beautiful but emotional also and I know that I can't obtain her so easily and if I want to enjoy with her then I have to poop also Well who will the person who leaves such a beautiful and gorgeous figure. ***'Yes you are right ben and both of them laugh'*** today I called her and I know that she likes me because I saw in her eyes that she fell ~~down~~ in my love and today she says yes to me But ben what happened if she came to know about you? So, what! who tells and when she came to know that this all thing was just a conspiracy till then it will be too late and till then I already will have revel with her after that she goes wherever she wants to go. But ben please also give me a chance to indulge with that girl ~~of course,~~ of course, Shane you are my best friend ***'Both of them laugh and suddenly Shane eyes goes to the door***

look somebody starring us' Ben stand and look behind us ***"He shocked"*** Lisa ***"Lisa came out from the room without saying any word".***

Ben how long she had been here? I don't know Shane maybe she listened to everything Go ben stop her and try to console her and said that nothing likes what you are thinking to go ben ***'Shane said forcefully'*** otherwise our whole plan is going to ~~be~~ perish Ben went but Lisa not listened to her and she left.

"Lisa came out from the hotel and she had totally broken and just thought one thing" what I listened that was the truth? I can't imagine that my own school's friend did this to me I thought Ben is a good guy but he has come evil oh! God now where I go.

"Lisa Bend down on the knees and start weeping loudly" the people started watching her and start gossiping about what happened to her ***'Suddenly one girl walked over there'*** what happened why the crowd gathers? Let us check ***"She went over there and saw that one girl cried very loudly"*** Hey what happened ***'Suddenly she shocked'*** Lisa is that you? What happened girl are you all right Lisa saw her and embrace her Michell Lisa – Lisa what happened why you sit like this and anything wrong with you come on! Stand up. ***'Michell stand Lisa and called taxi'*** Lisa tell me where we go '***Lisa whispered Jessica's house'*** ok let's go ***'Here in ~~the~~ Mr. Anderson's party Howard and Melisa reached over there'*** Hey! Howard Bryan Hey! How are you I am fine and what about you Bryan great Howard Hey meet ~~to~~ my wife Melisa hello Mr. Bryan how are you I am great you tell Mrs. Melisa are your husband keep you happy?

'Both of them laugh' No – No he always keep me happy and fulfill my all needs Great – Great so Howard don't you felt any trouble in- coming? no ~~Bryan~~, Bryan, you tell me where's your wife ~~actually~~ you know she didn't like ~~this~~ these parties and just want to ~~spent~~ spend all the time in the bar with her friends.

'Howard seems a little bit surprised oh!' look Mr. Anderson come over here Hello sir hello both of you I hope you enjoy the party yes of course sir so Bryan why your wife not came?

~~Actually~~ Mr. Anderson she had a headache that's why Ok – Ok and you Howard where's your wife here sir Meet Melisa, Melisa meet Mr. Anderson chairman of the company Nice to meet you Mr. Anderson you too Mrs. Midnight ok Howard you talked to Mr. Anderson I just look other employees ok Bryan.

'Bryan left' so Howard How's the party just amazing Mr. Anderson but where is your son he is not seen ~~in~~ at the party? ~~Actually~~ Howard, he doesn't like~~s~~ the parties and I insist him so much that today we will talk about your marriage and your presence must be over there but still, he said that who so ever you will choose its good for me you know eddy he always obey me and whatever the decision I take he always agreed that you are right Mr. Anderson the children should ~~be~~ obey their parent and it~~s~~ seems that you are lucky otherwise some children don't even think about their family's wishes at all ***'Howard speak quietly Melisa'*** yes you are right Mrs. Melisa I hope your daughter will also like my son.

Yes ~~Mr. Anderson~~, Mr. Anderson, my daughter is amazing and I proud that I am the dad of her and whatever the decision she takes I always support her because she is wise and she knows the difference between ~~the~~ right and wrong.

Yes – Yes Howard is right our daughter is rare Great! So, Howard can we talk ~~regarding~~ about the decision which you have to tell me? yes, Mr. Anderson, ~~actually~~ my daughter refused the proposal what! But Howard why?

Mr. Anderson, she loves somebody else and even I came to know this time and today she has gone on a date with that guy I am ~~really~~ sorry Mr. Anderson but I can't force my daughter I hope you understand ***"Mr. Anderson quiet for 2 minutes and said"*** now what can we do I ~~really~~ feel disappointed that – that's much of good relation ~~leaved~~ left from my hand. But you are right we can't force our children and one person not live happily then there is no meaning of this marriage ***'Mr. Anderson put a hand on Howard's shoulder'*** I give this bad news to my son I know he will get sad but I make him understand Thank you so much ~~Mr. Anderson,~~ Mr. Anderson, you light ~~a~~ weight from my heart it's all right Howard so enjoy the party.

'Here in Jessica's House Michelle and Lisa enter into the house' hey Jessica – Jessica ***'Jessica come down-stairs'*** hey Michelle but hey! Lisa is that you ***'Jessica shocked'*** what happened Lisa why you here! But you should have with ben? Lisa tell me! ***"Lisa was quiet"*** I got her outside the Hotel she was crying I asked so many times but she didn't tell me anything Hmm Jessica what happens what going on over here and Lisa you are here?

Dad, I don't know what happened with her I thought she would be on a date but Lisa why are you keep quiet Hmm I think we should take Lisa to the room first ok dad.

'Jessica took ~~the~~ Lisa into the room' sit Lisa now tell me something went wrong with you? ***"Lisa suddenly cried and embrace ~~to~~ Jessica"*** Lisa – Lisa why are you crying? ~~Actually,~~ Jessica ben cheated with me what! But he is your best-friend and he liked you then why he did this? He just wanted to misuse ~~of~~ me I reached earlier over there and I thought that I gave him a surprise~~d~~ but when I came to the room, I saw the room was open.

I thought he came to know about me so in thinking I went into the room and I hailed him but no reply came suddenly I listened the voices came from another room. When I saw him in ~~penetrate~~ penetrating then ben and his friend had been talking together about me that how he made me foolish and just want to enjoy with me and when he does ~~his~~ him all enjoyment then he leaves me. ***'Jessica got anger'*** how could he do that how could he played with somebody's emotion like this ***"We can't let them get away with this"*** Dad calls the police but what will happen if he ~~not opens~~does not open the mouth.

Don't worry Michelle when he sees the police he disgorge everything yes you are right Jessica I call the police right now.

No uncle, No Jessica please don't do this but why Lisa he did a frolic with you and you still I know but if I have gone to the police then it's come to the media and my family will be disgraced. Lisa every time you just think about this traducement ***"lest it to be late"***. No Jessica I will ~~definitely~~ do something but Lisa! No Jessica please don't force her I know why she said because she cares about her family and his reputation and being your father, I can understand the sorrow of Lisa but I also understand the world **"How Cruel He is"** he just blames only girls not boys and think what will happen in Lisa's house when he came to know about this.

Yes, Dad, you are right but we should do something of-course Sweetheart! When the right time will come, we all do something about this and Lisa is a wise girl and I know she will tell everything to her family ~~on~~ at a right time. Thanks, uncle, for your support I can't give pain to my *father* already he has lots of pressure and if I tell him this time then he might be not able to wreck.

Ok, Lisa as you want but make sure that you tell me everything otherwise I won't able to stop myself ok Jessica! Uncle, Jessica I have decided one thing what Lisa? **"I will do marry".**

What! Yes Jessica I accept that proposal which ~~were~~ was saying to me Lisa this is unfair you can't do this you will ruin your life no Jessica I always thought that I can ~~took~~ make my decision alone but now I ~~realise~~ realize that this was my biggest mistake ever and whatever the parent said that was right and I make a big mistake by disobeying them.

Now I won't do this again I shall be going tomorrow and say yes to him and my decision is final but Lisa what you said to him when they all will be asking about your date? I make any story Jessica It means you will say liar to him yes Jessica I said you this is not a right time and whenever I feel I shall tell everything but this time not.

'In early morning Jessica woke up and she saw that Lisa wasn't on the bed' Lisa- Lisa, where are you? **'she came out from the room and again**

called her name' Lisa! hey! Honey good morning Dad where is Lisa she is not in the room? ~~Actually,~~ Jessica Lisa left in the early ~~Morning~~morning. But where she is gone? And she doesn't need to tell me ~~no~~ any Jessica she said to me that she gets back to her house because it been a long time so I should go back.

But you couldn't stop her? How Jessica she wanted to go so how could I stop her and relax she is fine and if she will go to her house then she feels better I hope so Dad I will meet her later on.

'In Lisa's house, Howard was reading the newspaper and Lisa enter ~~into~~ the house' hello dad hey! Lisa my princess After all you remembered us! Yes, dad so how was your date, Lisa? I know- I know it is ~~really~~ awesome am I right? You don't know how much I feel happy today finally you get someone who loves me more than me. **'Melisa came out from the kitchen'** what going on over here? Oh! My sweet daughter came back hello mom you sit Lisa I bring a glass of water for you.

No Mom thanks but what happen Lisa you not look better everything is alright? You look tired and why not after all you were not sleeping the whole night your dad told me about your date so how was it? ~~Actually m~~Mom & dad I want to say something what say, Lisa? Dad, I accept your proposal and I want to do the marry. **'Howard shocked what!'** but why Lisa what happened is there any wrong with you? No Dad then Lisa! Ben did something wrong with you? no-no then what the reason Lisa? ~~Actually,~~ Dad, it was my mistake I thought Ben likes me and he called me to propose but it was not true.

He just wanted to be my friend and he loves someone else this was all just misunderstanding "**Howard grab her hand and said**" look at my eyes Lisa and say whatever you said it is true because I know my daughter, they can't do this type of mistake say true Lisa come on!

Don't worry about anything I am always with you No dad it's true it was just my misunderstanding nothing else.

'Melisa started thinking wow that's wonderful now I believed that ~~god~~ God **is with me'** well done Lisa you said so easily but now everything is finished your dad already refused to Mr. Anderson **'Howard sat down at the chair and said'** now ~~what~~ I will say to Mr. Anderson? And even I can't stand in front of him Lisa you ~~really~~ do a big mistake you should confirm~~ed~~ before say something now what I do?

'Melisa started thinking this is the right time to handle this situation' don't worry Howard I will talk to Mr. Anderson but how Melisa? Relax you just leave on me now and again children did the mistake and its parent responsibility to handle that and thinks about Lisa she is also a child so what happens if she did this mistake still there is no late, I go and talk to him and you see he will agree.

Lisa, you just go into her room and rest I know you didn't rest the whole night ok mom **'Lisa has gone into her room'** but Melisa how will you do that and what Mr. Anderson will think about us and if he refuses then what we shall do? Oh! My ~~innocence~~ innocent husband **"you don't know the power of women"** they can make anybody agreeable so what's their celebrity you just calm down and rest of the thing left on me.

Ok! Melisa do as you feel good but Howard you shouldn't scol~~de~~d Lisa like this, she is our daughter and everybody do mistakes and you didn't do any mistakes in your life **'Howard started thinking wow! Melisa so changed she act like her own mother'** you are right Melisa I go and talk to Lisa.

'here in the room, Lisa was thinking about her incident' I never thoughts that this thing would occur with me **"Every time I have always been Deceived and Deceived"** sometimes I think that **"why I became so beautiful that everybody just wants my body, not my ~~goodness~~ best and other things inside me"** they only want to do enjoy with me. But now it's over I will get marry and nobody can stare at me longer but today I feel delighted that mom supported me ~~in spite of~~despite dad its mean that now she has changed and finally understand my love and importance.

'Howard enter into the room' hey Lisa may I sit over here? Of-course dad you don't need to take any permission so dad you want to say something ~~actually~~ I am ~~really~~ sorry I rebuked you down. I shouldn't do this I should think it's just misunderstanding and everybody do this but when I listened that my ~~own~~ daughter did this who is so much wise then I couldn't able to control myself.

Lisa, please forgive me no dad it's not your fault every parent~~s~~ do this and you have the rights to Reprimand me no Lisa it's all my fault I used to expect a lot from you I just forgot that you are also a child and I wouldn't pay attention to you then who told you that what is right and wrong.

'Tears came from Howard's eyes' Lisa I love you so much and I can't see you in pain and if you have any trouble you can tell me don't think what I feel **"Lisa also started crying and hugged him".**

'In the **afternoon Melisa reached to the Mr. Anderson s' Mansion'** hello Mam whom you want to meet? Is Mr. Anderson in the house? Yes, mam, he is in the house you just wait I call him **'Melisa sat** ~~at~~ on **the sofa'**. Sir one lady wants to meet you ok I come in few minutes ok sir! mam, he comes in few minutes you just wait may I bring a glass of water for you? no thanks **'After 5minutes Anderson come downstairs'** oh! Good afternoon Mrs. Midnight you are here ~~how~~now?

Good afternoon Mr. Anderson I came here to talk ok-ok please sit is there anybody? Yes sir! Please bring two cups of coffees for us ok sir with sugar or without? a little bit and bring Italian sweet also along with them. So Mrs. Midnight tell me what do you want to say? ~~Actually, i~~It's ~~really~~ awkward but before say anything I am ~~really~~ sorry but why Mrs. Midnight?

You didn't do anything no Mr. Anderson we did but now I have come to fix here sir your two coffees and Italian sweet have it Mrs. Melisa thank you so much you also have it ~~Mr. Anderson of course~~, Mr. Anderson of course, Mrs. Midnight. So, what did you said Mrs. Midnight? ~~actually~~ I want to talk to you regarding the marriage of my daughter and your son what! Mrs. Midnight you just say elucidate ~~actually~~ my daughter agreed to marry to your son.

What! But Howard said that she likes somebody else and she didn't do the marriage then? ~~Actually~~ Mr. Anderson, it's all my daughter's fault she got some misunderstanding that he likes her but he liked somebody else. She told this time even Howard got shocked when she gave this news but you understand that children are ~~innocence~~ innocent and she all did this thing in the darkness.

So please I request you to again think about its Mrs. Melisa this thing is fine but what will I say to my son? I already said no to him and you don't know how much he feels bad when he will listen about it and marriage is not a game whenever you want to quit and whenever you want to come back my son is emotional and when somebody hurt its emotion then he not able to tolerate them.

Sorry, Mrs. Midnight but I can't do this if you do it again then what shall I do? **'Melisa started thinking the situation is going from my hand I will do something'** oh! Mr. Anderson you behave like a child I am not ~~force~~ forcing you but just think about it if you refuse this proposal then you get any other good proposal like this and what Howard will think about you? that Mr. Anderson can't forgive my one mistake and as far as I know your son he is so sincere, charming and will they get any other girl like my daughter? She is so smart, sincere and obeys the elders and one of the most important things that she is the most beautiful in whole London.

And one more thing I have to say please don't mind **"Nobody is so pure you know very well"** everybody does the mistake ones in our life or many times rest I said you earlier also I can't force you to rest it's your choice. **'Melisa stood up'** I told what I wanted to say but please you think about it lest later on, you regret ~~on~~ your decision ok Mr. Anderson thank you so much to give me your valuable time bye.

'Melisa started going to the door and here Mr. Anderson thinks' she is ~~absolutely~~ right I don't get this type of proposal ever and so what! If she did a mistake then everybody does the mistake what's a big deal in this, she is the only one who handles my son and will take out from that grief which ~~were~~ was given by that girl.

Wait! Mrs. Midnight you don't need to go I have decided I accept your proposal I understand now that we can't judge anybody ~~on the basis of~~ based on one mistake thank you so much Mrs. Midnight. **'Melisa started thinking plan successful'** it's ok Mr. Anderson I feel glad that you understood everything.

So, when do you come to our house with your son? I am not deciding this time but before this, I will talk to my son then I tell you ok Mr. Anderson as you want so Mrs. Midnight on this time there must be a small party what you say? Ok, Mr. Anderson! alright please bring two champagne and two glass.

"The champagne and two glass came and the noise of pop-up come and both of them celebrated but who knows what this celebration will bring in Lisa s' life."

'In Lisa s' house,' Howard was thinking what happen she ~~not ea~~did not come back something happened over there? what Mr. Anderson would ~~said~~ say to her? I think he would say no to her and why not after all he is a big man and they loves his reputation more than his children.

'Howard was thinking on that time Melisa enter into the house' hey! Howard Melisa, you came back are you alright? Wait I go and bring a glass of water for you no-no Howard I am fine and you don't need to go anywhere you just sit down with me.

So, Melisa what happened over there did he agreed? Yes, he has agreed what! But Melisa I can't believe how you did this?

I told you- you don't know the power of women that's why women always win the heart of men you are right Melisa as like you win my heart oh! Come on Howard why are you joking? No, seriously I say true. Alright-alright so where are both of them? ~~Actually,~~ Melisa Lisa and Adam ~~gone~~ went outside I said Adam to take Lisa for wandering so that Lisa s' mood will get fresh.

That s' great Howard but Melisa you didn't tell me how you made him agreed? Nothing I just said that we can't judge anybody ~~on the basis of~~based on one mistake and it~~s~~ all happened in misunderstanding simple great Melisa! **It is agreeing that 'you can change anybody s' mind'**.

Thanks, Howard I feel glad that you are happy now my daughter s' life will ~~totally~~ change and she will get lots of happiness hmm Melisa! So, when do they come to our house? ~~Actually, h~~He said that he will talk to his son then tell us. I hope his son agrees! I don't think so Melisa but why Howard? You don't know his son Melisa he is a stubborn guy and he not listens to anybody his father agreed but may-be his son does not agree ~~for~~ with this.

'In Anderson s' Mansion Eddy enter into the house' dad-dad, where are you? what happen sir do you have any trouble? He called me and from their voice its look like that he was in trouble that s' why I came rapidly. Do you know where is he? Yes, sir, he is in the bedroom and the doctor is also with them what! What happens to him? ~~Actually,~~ ~~h~~He got unconscious and fell ~~down~~ from the stairs.

'Eddy got hesitate and ran to the room and he enters into the room and said' dad are you all right? **'Anderson lied on a bed and** the **doctor was checking him'** doctor what happened to my dad? ~~Actually,~~ ~~h~~He had some kind of stress and in this, he didn't eat anything because of this thing happened. But I don't understand what kind of stress he has? I don't know Mr. Eddy but you shall take care of him otherwise their situation can get ~~more~~ worse.

No, I won't let this happen doctor good Mr. Eddy I wrote some medicine on prescription give it at time ok doctor thank you so much you save his life no Eddy this is my work. **'doctor had gone and Eddy sat near the Anderson'** and **'After sometime Anderson s' conscious back'** Eddy how are you, my son? **'Eddy in rejoicing'** Dad are you alright? Of course, my son when I have a good son like you ~~than~~ then what can happen to me but dad how you got unconscious and what kind of stress you have? Come on tell me?

Son, I always worry about you that after me who will care of you? I know after your mom how I grew you. You spent many nights without me, celebrated your birthday alone, and even did your homework by own self and I just only busy in-built my empire.

But I always kept everything in my mind every night when you slept, I came and

Saw you without your knowing and every birthday before you awaken, I kept present for you and you remembered why your teacher not chided you? yes dad I remembered this is because son before you reach to school, I reached over there and told everything that s' why he never Blustered on you.

Or you say that you threaten him, right dad!

Yes-yes Eddy '**both of them laugh**' Eddy

I can't see your sad face I can do anything for you and you are my whole life I know dad but you didn't tell me the reason behind your tension? Eddy, I want that you ~~do~~ to marry. What! But dad I told you that I don't want to marry then why you force me so much I want to spend my whole life ~~in~~ enjoying and stay alone rather than become a care~~-~~taker or a baby sitter.

I know my son but how much it will be going on? One day you have to take my seat because you are an heir of this company and this house and all thing is belonging to you.

I all build this through my hard work~~-~~ and it all just for you and I can't see you ~~to~~ ruin your life like this Eddy you are my biggest responsibility try to understand my son ' **Anderson in weep'** if happen~~-~~ something to you then I will kill myself.

No ~~dad~~, dad, you are everything for me ok fine if you are happy in this ~~than~~ then **"I ready for marriage"** oh! That's great my son you don't know by saying this how much happiness you give to me Now you see how I ~~organise~~ organize your marriage and reception~~-~~ ~~Afterall~~, After all, it's Anderson s' son's Marriage the whole of London is going to see that.

'In early morning' very good doctor you did a great job I never knew that you are a great actor also! no Mr. Anderson you told me to do that s' why I did this but what will happen if your son came to know about this? You don't need to worry about this doctor you just mind your own business sorry Mr. Anderson this was not my meaning Relax doctor I am just joking ok tell me have you got your fees? Of course, Mr. Anderson ~~on~~ at the same time the fees reached in my account ok I talk to you later on.

'Anderson cut the call and called to Howard' hello its Howard s' Residence hello Mrs. Melisa it~~s~~ me Anderson oh, Mr. Anderson, how are you? I am fine and you tell Mrs. Melisa? I am great but why you call in the early morning? Howard is sleeping wait I wake him up.

No-no Mrs. Midnight I want to talk to you ~~actually~~ I have a piece of great news for you **"My son agrees** ~~for~~ to **marriage"** what! Wow, that's ~~really~~ delightful Mr. Anderson finally you made him agreed on yes-yes and I want to say that ~~me~~ I and my son today come to your house for the meet to your daughter and we shall talk about the marriage preparation also that s' wonderful Mr. Anderson I awake Howard and give this good news, ok Mrs. Midnight have a nice day.

Howard-Howard wake up there is good news! what happens Melisa why you shout and what s' good news? Mr. Anderson s's son get agreed ~~for~~ to the marriage what did you said Melisa that s' true? Of course, I am not saying a lie Mr. Anderson called and gave this news to me. I ~~really~~ surprise how its son agrees on this? Might be Mr. Anderson did something oh! Leave it Howard what we have to do! You just think it's the time of happiness.

We have to do lots of preparation they can reach anytime what! ~~are~~ have they come to our house, Melisa? Yes, Howard so we should do hurry I go and wake up both of them and you go down and wipe the whole house ok Howard. Lisa, Adam wakes up both of you fast what happens, dad? Come on Adam wake up today boy s' family come to see Lisa what! yes, Lisa today they come to see you.

You go and get ready when do they come, dad? They can come anytime Adam ok-ok Adam you get ready fast you must be there when they come ok dad.

'After 1-hour Howard moved here and there ~~in~~ is **hesitation'** Melisa what are you doing? Look at the time and you still not get ready just give me a 5-minutes Howard I go into the room and get ready come on Melisa do fast! **'Suddenly the doorbell rang'** wait I come **'Howard open the door'** Hello Mr. Anderson, hello Eddy. Hello, Uncle please come **'Both of them enter** ~~into~~ **the house and sat** ~~at~~ on **the sofa'** Melisa please bring two glasses of water so Mr. Anderson didn't you have any trouble in coming? No Howard we came comfortably so you tell Howard, how are you? I am fine Sir and Eddy what about you how is your study going? Great uncle.

Hello Mr. Anderson, Hello Mrs. Midnight, how are you? I am great and what about you Mr. Anderson? I am good Eddy this is Howard s' wife and Mrs. Melisa this is Eddy my son Hello Mrs. Midnight, Hello Eddy. You are so smart and handsome Eddy thanks Mrs. Melisa for your compliment Howard where s' your daughter? 1 minutes Sir Melisa go and take Lisa with you, Lisa! **'Eddy and Anderson get a little bit surprised by listening to this name'** here Sir my daughter Lisa.

"She gets shocked by seeing him, Eddy!" "And here Eddy and Anderson also get shocked and Eddy said, Lisa!"

'Eddy stood up from the sofa and gone into the room' what happens Mr. Anderson why he ~~gone~~ went like that? I don't know Howard but Melisa? I think Howard ~~he~~ gets shy I go into the room and look at him but Mr. Anderson are you sure? Of course, Howard you just wait until we come in few minutes. **"Anderson has also gone into the room and here Lisa didn't understand anything and she was thinking what is happening here will I do marry with Eddy when I know that what he did with me?"**

I never knew that my father works in his father s' company and Mr. Anderson is the boss of my father but what I do? I can't do anything if I said or refuse this proposal then there will be a great insult of my father in ~~the~~ front of Mr. Anderson but how can I live with that guy? Who doesn't care about anything **'Here in Room'** Eddy-Eddy! **'Eddy in anger'** just answer me dad one thing did you know about this? Did you know that Lisa is the daughter of Howard?

Come on Dad speak? No, my son, I swear I didn't know that Lisa is the girl of Howard I came to know this time but dad how can I marry ~~with~~ this girl?

Who ruined my life, gave me grief and sorrow, and insulted me in front of my friend I always thought one day I shall take my revenge and break down the ego of her beauty, and from that incident occurred with me I have been burning in vengeance.

"Living with this girl it's good that I am going to die" dad you just go outside and say no to him you always being stupid Eddy you never think from your mind this is the time when you can appease your vengeance. Just think if you marry ~~with~~ that girl then you can do anything nobody can't stop you and have you thought about why Lisa

~~not said~~did not say anything to her dad & mom ~~till~~? because they are afraid that their reputation will get down and we can take benefit of this fear and by this, you can easily take your revenge and she will ~~can't~~ speak a single word in front of us.

By this marriage, your revenge will get fulfilled and you don't know I also burnt in that flame in which you were burning ~~on~~ at that time when I saw tears in your eyes because of this girl I had been also waiting for this kind of moment. And as you can see god is also with us when they give us such a wonderful chance then why not we take the benefit of this! you are right dad thanks you open my eyes **"Now you see Lisa how I make your Life Deteriorate".**

'Both of them came outside from the room' what happen eddy why you went like this? No Mrs. Midnight I told you eddy got shy because your daughter is so beautiful that anybody can shy Thanks a lot Mr. Anderson I think we should leave the children alone for a while so that they do know each other properly and ~~its very important that they~~they must know each other's interest also before the marriage what you say, Howard? You are right Mr. Anderson let's go outside and have a sweet dish ~~to~~ at the near sweet shop.

'Howard, Melisa, and Anderson ~~gone~~ went **outside and Eddy & Lisa alone in the house'** Lisa I know after saw me you don't want to do marry and it is obvious after all I did a very wrong with you **"Lisa say in a belly rag"** so now you understand this just tell me what's a conspiracy behind this? I know you can't loyal ~~with~~ to anybody and now you have got a chance to play with my life yes Mr. Eddy! Lisa, I understand your anger and you have the right~~s~~ to blame me but after this incident seriously I have been not sleeping few nights in guilty I always thought that why I did this with you? ~~actually~~ I was tempted Lisa I know there is no forgiveness for this mistake which I have done.

But I want to say sorry to you because I still love you and I vow that this mistake will be ~~never~~ never-repeating again but I can't force you to do marry ~~with~~ me.

If you want to refuse this ~~marry~~ marriage then you can say No to my Dad I will make him understand but one thing I want to say that whatever the decision of yours I will love you forever.

"Lisa was in big confusion" what I do now? Should I believe ~~on~~ in him? May-be he says true but how could I forget that what he did with me? but he said so confidently that it did not look like that he says liar Now I don't have any other choice if I say anything then there will be No reputation left of my family and what Mr. Anderson will think about me? He is a great guy and he always supported me and today their child ~~is only change~~only changes because of him I think everybody should get a chance to improve himself then why not Eddy?

'Eddy stood outside and Lisa came out from the house'

Eddy I have decided I marry ~~to~~ you I give you a chance to change yourself I also love you; I hope you will not break my believe again oh! Thanks, Lisa you don't know by this I get a new life now you see I will always keep you happy **'here Howard, Melisa and Anderson came back'.** So, children how were you~~r~~ talking I hope both of you would have known something about each other yes Mr. Anderson I like eddy and I want to do marry ~~with~~ him.

Great! Lisa so it~~s~~ is decide that marriage will be after two days on 25th September **"Howard shocked and said 2 days"** what happen Howard Is there any problem? No Mr. Anderson but how can we arrange everything in 2 days I mean how it will happen? Oh! Come on Howard I will arrange everything you don't need to worry when both of the children get ready then why we do delay You just only take your daughter to the church nothing else and we shall keep the reception on the same day.

Ok Mr. Anderson as you like ok Howard, we meet him in marriage come on! Eddy **'Both of them gone and Howard, Melisa, and Lisa came inside'** Dad I am going into the room but why? Are you all right? Yes, dad just a little bit tired ok Lisa you go. **'Lisa has gone into the room'** Howard today I feel so happy I can't tell you after all now our dream come true, I will buy new clothes.

"Howard looks in tension" what happen Howard you did not seem happy ha – Nothing Melisa I just thought that this happened so fast hmm you are right Howard but think now the happiness comes in our daughter's life whatever the grief she saw in her life now there is an end of him so you just relax and focus on this.

'Jessica reached to ~~the~~ Wanda's house' Wanda – Wanda, where are you? wait I am coming come on fast! Wanda, I have to tell you something what happen Jessica why are you shouting? Do you know that Lisa is doing marry **'Wanda shocked'** with whom? Eddy! What! are you joking aren't you? no, I am not joking its true Wanda but who told you,

Jessica? ~~Actually, o~~One of my friends listened to eddy talking with their friends he said that he was also looking happy.

Why not ~~he~~ be happy after all he succeeds in what he wants to achieve but Jessica what happens to Lisa why she going to ~~be~~ have perished her life? She knows that eddy was the one who did a wrong with him. I think Wanda her parents force him to do marry ~~with~~ that guy because eddy is a wealthy guy and you know that he is the son of Mr. Anderson what! Anderson but he is a wealthy guy in the whole London and eddy is his son that's a surprise but as far as I know Lisa s' father, he is not like that.

But Wanda we should do something about it we save Lisa at any cost don't worry Jessica we not let this marriage happen **"At night before the marriage Howard enter ~~into the~~ Lisa's room"** Lisa are you sleeping? Dad is that you? I thought that Adam comes sorry I didn't want to disturb you no dad you did not disturb me and I always feel happy when you with me.

Hmm! Lisa, I want to talk I know whatever ~~the~~ happens here it's going to be fast but for me, there is nothing more than your gladness so I want to ask one thing please say me true **"Howard grab Lisa's hand are you**

happy with this marriage?" "Lisa quiet for a second and said" of course dad where I will get this proposal like any other proposal, I know but I don't want to impose anything on you or force you to do marry so please tell ~~you~~ me not to hide anything from me? Come on! Dad, what you are saying? I said that I am happy and if anything inside me then I ~~definitely~~ tell~~s~~ you but there is nothing like this so dad you just relax and sleep tomorrow is a big day for both of us.

How can I relax when I know that tomorrow **"I give my piece of heart to somebody"** ok Lisa you now sleep **"Howard** has **gone and Lisa started crying"** how can I tell you ~~dad~~, dad, why I do this marriage because I care about your and respect more than

me.

"In early morning Lisa was wearing her bridal dress and Howard was waiting outside" Lisa how much time you take come on! My princess we have already late for the marriage everybody would be waiting over there yes dad just 5 minutes **"After 5 minutes Lisa came out** ~~from~~ of **the room"** dad! "**she hails" "Howard gets surprised to her"** ~~wow~~ Wow Lisa! you look absolutely princess today.

You are looking *fantastic*, stunning and one *of* the most important things that **"you ~~are~~ look like your mother when she wore this dress she was looking same like you" "Howard started crying and sat down"** dad what happen? nothing Lisa today I ~~realise~~ realize that **"How much this day is so beautiful and painful".**

Today your mom will ~~really~~ get happy wherever she will yes dad you are right today I miss her so much I wish she is today with us don't feel sad Lisa your mom always with you in your heart and their memories can never be stolen by anybody yes dad by the way you also look stunning today oh! Come on don't joke with me. No dad seriously you are looking handsome **'Both of them laugh'** Ok – Ok Lisa let's go everybody is waiting over there.

'In the church, everybody was waiting and Eddy stood in front of the father and he asked about the bridal' where she is? It's almost time if she not come at the time then the right time of prayer will be gone no Father I just go outside and ask her mother about him where they are? **'Anderson came outside from the church'** Mrs. Midnight where ~~is~~ are Howard and Lisa? the Prayer s' time is going yes Mr. Anderson I know but I also have been waiting for him **'then only the car came and Lisa &Howard came out from the car'.**

Here both of them Lisa, Howard why were you getting so late? Sorry Melisa ~~actually~~ Lisa was ready but I was not ready yet ok Howard but Lisa you look Stunning in this bridal ~~Dress~~ dress today. Thanks, mom yes Mrs. Midnight our Daughter ~~is look~~looks like a **"once in a blue moon"** thanks to Mr. Anderson alright Lisa you come inside Eddy and Father ~~is~~ are waiting for you **'Howard, Lisa, and Anderson gone inside the church'.**

Ok, everything is alright now I shall also go inside **'suddenly somebody hailed her name Mrs. Melisa' 'Melisa moved back and saw that Wanda and Jessica** ~~was~~ were **coming'** hello Mrs. Melisa, hello both of you I just thought that **where** were you both? Now come to the prayer ~~is almost start~~almost starts. No ~~Mrs. Melisa~~, Mrs. Melisa, we can't attend this marriage yes Wanda is right we can't but why Wanda and Jessica? You are the best friend ~~of~~ her then?

~~Actually~~ Mrs. Melisa, we have to say something please stop the marriage what! are you out of your mind Wanda what are you saying? I know but this marriage will ruin everything but how can you say that Wanda? ~~Actually~~ Mrs. Melisa, you don't know the incident which was occurred with ~~the~~ Lisa what Incident Jessica? Please say elucidate actually at the time of Christmas **"Eddy was forcefully tried to physical with Lisa".**

What! what did you said, Jessica? Yes Mrs. Melisa Jessica is right Eddy and Lisa know each other at the beginning of ~~the~~ college they were good friends but Eddy s' resentment was not good at all for Lisa they just wanted to misuse ~~of~~ her. And the date on which she went "**ben turns out to be like Eddy, his motives were not noble"** that was good Lisa listened to everything and she came to know about his intentions otherwise what happened? We can't imagine.

Please Mrs. Melisa we both Request you stop this marriage and save ~~the~~ Lisa s' life if you say then we go inside and tell everything to her father, no I mean there is no need ~~of~~ for that I tell everything to Howard thank you so much to both of you- you show your true friendship. Now it's my turn to show ~~my~~ the true love I just go and stop this ok Mrs. Melisa we just leave it up to **you 'both of them gone and Melisa get happy'** today I believe ~~on~~ in god he is with me I always thought that how I take revenge for my insult?

But it seems that **"it will be taken by somebody"** what these girls thought that I shall go and reveal everything what a stupid both of her they are

Credulous like Lisa thanks Eddy you don't know "**you will become my way to take a revenge from her"**

"Melisa laughed and came back to church and she didn't say anything and let this marriage happened".

'**In the evening after the reception, Eddy and Lisa stood outside and preparing for going to Anderson s' house'** so Howard now on Lisa is my responsibility you don't think much about her. Yes, Mr. Anderson but I am her father and how can I leave my responsibility like this Eddy I hope you keep my daughter happy of course dad you don't need to take any tension of this and Lisa stay happy and call me always and don't forget your father no dad not at all "**Lisa started crying and hugged to Howard"** now you just go and **"Howard gently pushed Lisa" " Lisa and Eddy sat into the car and both of them gone and Howard started crying and Melisa tried to console him"**.

"It had been six months lots of things happened with Lisa and she suffered a lot and one day she sat near the window and looked outside a white pigeon came and sat on the pole and by seeing him she started thinking".

What a life of this pigeon? He is looking so beautiful and there is no pain, no grief, no sorrow and no cheat in their life.

I thought that now I would get a better life and he has also changed but I was wrong I can't imagine what I suffered in this six month and the most worse thing is that his father is also like that all the time I got cheated, endured pain just because of this beauty.

But now I can't face anymore **"I also want to fly just like this pigeon and want to go that place where everybody loves each other and not only see** the **beauty of outside but also of inside".**

"but before I do this, I want to ~~apologise~~ apologize for **my all mistakes and reveal everything which I concealed from my dad and after this, she wrote a letter".**

sorry, dad I know after this may be, I am not with you but you are my hero and I always love you please forgive me **"And after this, she stood up at the window and** ~~leapt~~ leaped **from that".**

“Lisa fell ~~down~~ **on the ground and blood came out** ~~form~~ from **their head and her eyes opened and** the **small smile on her face and she saw that pigeon also flew”.**

“Here one of the servants saw this and screamingly chant to the Mansion”

‘In Mansion both of them was drinking’ hey dad today my close friend will come and they want enjoyment oh, don’t worry my son we have the thing of fun yes-yes, I go and say Lisa to dress well. Mr. Anderson~~-~~‘s **servant** ~~in~~ **screams’** what happen why you gasped like that? Sir Mrs. Lisa! what servant? She has committed suicide. What! **‘Anderson shocked’** are you say true? Yes, sir, I saw from my eyes **‘he sat down in shocked’** hey dad where is Lisa have you seen her? Dad, what happens why you sit like this and you look ~~hesitate~~hesitant?

Son Lisa ~~gone~~ went she has committed suicide what! ‘Eddy shocked too’ how is possible she didn’t have anything then Sir she fell ~~down~~ from the window I can’t believe this how can she do that? Dad now what we will be doing? You don’t need to worry son Mr. Anderson **‘Another servant**

came inside' the police have come what! who has called the police? **OH! My god and 'Anderson and Eddy ran outside'**.

'Here in Lisa s' house' it's been a long time she hadn't called me I think that she forgets me oh! Come on Howard now she has a big responsibility and they have to look after another house also but Melisa I spoke 3month ago and since they have not received a call till date.

Oh! Howard dad here is your call thanks Adam Hello **"Howard listened** to **something and suddenly phone drop from their hand"**

Howard what happens? yes, dad come on tell us? Lisa! **"She did suicide"** what! **"Melisa shocked"** Howard what you say?

No – No Lisa you can't do this with me you can't leave me like this **"And by saying this Howard ran away" "He reached** ~~to the~~ **Anderson's house lots of crowds stood over there and the photographer** ~~were~~ was **taking the photograph"**.

Howard pushed everybody and came over there where ~~the~~ Lisa's body kept, he is totally broken and bent down on knees and very loudly called her name Lisa! he started crying loudly and everybody started looking at him and whispering together who is he? And mean-while, Melisa and Adam also reached over there.

"Both of them also started crying and Melisa asked ~~from~~ Anderson" how ~~is it happened~~does it happen? I don't know Mrs. Midnight Lisa was always happy and they were not seeming like that she was ~~in~~ under some kind of stress.

"Then only one of the police officers came and gave one piece of paper to the senior" sir before she does suicide, she left some kind of letter ~~on~~ in the name of Howard.

"As Howard listened to this he got up and grab the piece of paper from their hand and he opens the letter and started reading"

"In the letter, she wrote": -

"Hello dad I knew when you will get this letter may be I shall not with you I must have gone far away from you but I always love you and I always respect you and you will be my hero always dad I know you never forgive me for my this mistake but I couldn't do anything I was tired of all this conspiracy, deceive and cheat. Dad, I always concealed many things from you because I thought that by this I would able to save your reputation but I didn't know that by this I just put you in the darkness you always said me whatever the problem you have just share with me

and even my friends also said me to tell everything true. But I always kept quiet but now I ~~realise~~ realize that it was my biggest mistake~~s~~ if I told you earlier ~~then~~ than maybe today, I am with you. but now it's time to tell you each and everything dad for this suicide Eddy and his father ~~is~~ are responsible. After the marriage all the time Eddy and his father torched me, always beating me, and even never gave me ~~a~~ proper food Eddy all the time forced me to lie~~d~~ with their friends and when I refused her, he beat me. And one thing I want to tell that I knew ~~the~~ Eddy earlier and he was the one who did ~~a~~ wrong ~~with~~ to me at the time of the Christmas party. I also told everything about him to his father ~~on~~ at that time he pretended like that he is very well-wisher and rebuked him but after the marriage my this illusion also got broke and you will remember~~ed~~ that I went on a date and you asked ~~that~~ him why you refused this proposal. Because ben was also like that, he just wanted to misuse ~~of~~ me and just want to fulfill their desire he made ~~a~~ plannings with his one friend that's why he did a friendship with me. Dad I know I should tell you all this thing earlier but I was afraid that if I told you then what's your reaction and what people will think about us? But you always love me truly, you always care for me and supported me and you never care about the world and despite ~~of~~ this still, I not understood your feeling and emotion.

Dad I never knew that "My ~~own~~ beauty will become my enemy".

Dad, I say sorry to you but now I want to go far away from this but I always stay in your heart. "And I pray to god that every daughter gets a father like you but never get a so much beauty like me".

Your princess

Lisa

"After reading this Howard get outrageous and he grabbed the collar of the eddy and started beating him"

How dare you how you touched my daughter? I will not leave you **"Melisa tried to stop him but she won't able to stop" "Howard started to threaten Anderson"** now you see I won't let you get away with this you will pay for this. Then only Jessica and Wanda reached over there and both of them started crying by seeing her Wanda I always warned her to tell everything but she never listened to me. But hey! Mrs. Melisa when we told you everything then why you ~~not stopped~~did not stop the marriage?

What! yes Mr. Howard we told everything to Mrs. Melisa at the time of marriage Melisa **"Howard in anger"** says true! Were these girls told you everything? Yes, Howard **"Howard slapped on Melisa's face"** after all you show your personality of stepmother tell me what I ~~not ga~~did not give you house, money and what my daughter did with you? she always believed ~~on~~ in you, always love you and what you give to her in return **"Death"** No I can't tolerate you anymore officer I file a case against these three people please give him a strong punishment. Don't worry Mr. Howard we give him ~~a~~ that type of punishment which these will never forget and after all, we also have proof.

"Officer takes away Melisa eddy and Anderson to the jail and Howard bent down on the floor and started crying again in near of Lisa's body and their friends crying too".

"After 1 year three of them get a punishment of spending a whole life in jail and after that Howard leave the London and staying in America with his son but his heart always cried for Lisa".

Conclusion

Lisa like many girls till today facing these types of problems Every girl wants to get beautiful and want to become more attractive and there is no wrong ~~in~~ with that. But beautiful from inside is more important than beautiful from outside we can't change ~~each and~~ every people of the way of seeing but if they want ~~than~~ then ~~each and~~ every people can change their way of seeing by himself but it's not easy in today's time and because of this we don't know when for any girl **"their beauty become their ~~own~~ enemy".**

Hello everybody meet my real inspiration of my life My Dad, My heart, My hero and My best friend. By the way I don't have words for him to explain but still I want to say few about him he is unique and have a most beautiful and kind hearted person. He always supported me in my all troubles and he did for us beyond the limits I still not agreed he is not with me but have to believe. He did a great struggle in his life and today what I am because of my dad.

Thank you dad for all your supports and bless me that I can take your name to the very top.

❤I LOVE YOU MY DAD❤

www.ingramcontent.com/pod-product-compliance
Lightning Source LLC
Chambersburg PA
CBHW050019170726
48282CB00025B/467
9788194907671